THE ROAD TO WINTER

Mark Smith lives on Victoria's Surf Coast with his family. *The Road to Winter* is his first book.

THE ROAD TO WINTER

MARK SMITH

TEXT PUBLISHING MELBOURNE AUSTRALIA

textpublishing.com.au

The Text Publishing Company
Swann House
22 William Street
Melbourne Victoria 3000
Australia

First published in Australia by The Text Publishing Company, 2016
Reprinted 2016

Cover and page design by Imogen Stubbs
Shed photograph by Rowena Naylor / Stocksy
Bush photograph by Dominique Felicity Chapman / Stocksy
Typeset by J&M Typesetters

Printed in Australia by Griffin Press, an Accredited ISO AS/NZS
14001:2004 Environmental Management System Printer

National Library of Australia Cataloguing-in-Publication entry
Author: Smith, Mark.
Title: The road to winter / by Mark Smith.
ISBN: 9781925355123 (paperback)
ISBN: 9781922253712 (ebook)
Dewey Number: A823.3

For all those who have sought refuge,
only to be met by closed hearts.

1

The wind's picked up off the strait again, whistling hard and sharp through the coastal wattles. The bay has turned to white caps all the way out to the open ocean. The weather will force me and Rowdy indoors, laying low and huddling together for warmth. We can't risk a fire for fear of the smoke being seen.

But at least now I've got time to take stock after the last few days of hunting and fishing.

I get the rabbit traps out of the shed and oil the springs and plates, then run the chains through a greasy rag to keep them from rusting up. My hands are soon black with grime. There are big calluses on the palms and half-circles of dirt under my nails.

After two winters on my own I've almost given up trying to stay clean. Sometimes when I walk past the mirror in the bathroom I hardly recognise myself. My hair's long and matted, bleached by the sun, and my face is usually peeling—either from the wind or sunburn. I've tried hacking at my hair with scissors, but I think it made it worse. Once a month or so I heat water for a proper wash, but mostly I just rinse off in the ocean.

Angowrie is deserted now, all the shops cleaned out and most of the houses stripped of anything useful. Before the virus, when the town was still a town, we thought our isolation would save us. We were two hours drive from the city, a little town with a pub, a couple of churches and shops all lined up and looking out to sea. Early on, when we still believed it would all blow over, we followed the news reports and daily updates about quarantine areas. The health authorities tried to reassure everyone they had it under control, but when the hospitals were locked down and law and order fell away, people started panic-buying.

And there was the weather. I was only thirteen then, but even I could see it changing: the summers longer, the winters shorter, the ocean staying warmer right through the autumn. The storms came more regularly, the king tides pushing right up the river valley and flooding the houses that used to sit well clear of the water. Up until the internet went down for good and all the communications fell away—phones, radio, everything—there were theories flying around about how the warmer climate was making everyone sick.

The main road into town was barricaded and patrols were set up to stop people coming from the north. But they came anyway, finding their way down through the bush tracks to somewhere they thought would be safer.

That's probably how the virus reached us.

At first, I didn't really understand the seriousness of it. I was happy we didn't have to go to school. All summer I'd been dreading moving to Wentworth High, not because I didn't like school, but because it was so big and different and new.

And, of course, I'd always copped shit for my voice.

For years I had problems talking; I couldn't seem to form the words properly. It was like trying to talk with a mouth full of sand, so mostly I just stayed quiet. Mum and Dad could understand me well enough, and Rowdy too.

I didn't know it at the time, but everything I learned back then would help me survive. For as long as I could remember I'd hunted rabbits up on the edge of the farmland, dived off the point for abalone and caught crays in season. I knew every nook and cranny of the tea trees along the dunes and every trail and bike track through the bush. I understood the weather patterns like they were part of me. The big westerlies that pushed up the swell, the southerlies that brought the chill up from Antarctica and, in summer, the northerlies that blew heat down off the inland.

Outside, the wind has turned to rain, beating on the iron roof. Rowdy sits at my feet and rests his face on his paws.

He likes it when I lift my foot and scratch him on his belly. I got Rowdy as pup when I was ten. He's a bitser, but somewhere back in his line Dad reckoned there must have been some dingo. He's lean and strong and always on the lookout for a rabbit to chase down. We're a team, the two of us. Before the virus we did things together just for fun—now we do them to stay alive.

Later in the afternoon the rain eases and I decide to check out the beach. The wind's backed off and the river mouth will be getting some protection. It sounds pretty stupid to say that I still surf whenever I can, but once I'd worked out how to survive, how to hunt, grow some veggies and forage in the forest, I knew I needed something more. Something that kept me in touch with my old life. It's dangerous, not because of anything in the water but because of what's on the land—who might arrive in town while I'm caught up enjoying myself. But it's a risk that's worth taking to stay sane.

Rowdy watches me put on my old raincoat, and straight-away he knows what's up. He jumps to his feet and waits by the back door until I've pulled on my boots.

We scout through the stand of sheoaks at the back of the house, cross Parker Street and make our way into the thick tea trees at the back of the dunes, following the tracks and tunnels to the base of the lookout at the river mouth.

From the top I can see all the way back up to the bridge. I check for movement. For two winters there's been nothing, but I know, one day, the Wilders will come looking for food or fuel or people.

I keep my board and wetsuit hidden up here under the

platform. The sets are lining up and peeling off into the river mouth. The sky is clear to the west so I take a chance on getting a few waves before the next storm front hits.

It always feels good to be out in the water, looking back at the town and the ridge beyond it. Rowdy prowls up and down the beach, chasing seagulls and sniffing the wind for danger.

The river mouth is my favourite wave, breaking hard and fast on the bar and barrelling all the way to the shore break.

I get half-a-dozen good rides before the sky darkens again and I decide to make my way in.

Rowdy's waiting in the shallows and he dances around my legs as we head back up to the platform. I change quickly, the cold wind biting at my skin, and stash my board and wetsuit.

With the last of the light fading behind the next big storm-head, we make our way back down into the tea trees, Rowdy running ahead now, eager for the warmth of his blanket in the corner of the kitchen.

Out of habit, I look at Sarah Watford's place as I cross Parker Street, thinking that one day she'll be there, standing on the front porch in her school dress and waving me over. But the screen door is still hanging by one hinge, the windows are still smashed and the path is still overgrown. Time to get home.

Even when the virus was spreading beyond the cities, everyone in town thought they'd find a drug to kill it off, that the government would sort things out and we'd all go back to the way we were before.

Right up until the day Jim Sackville's supermarket was trashed, I thought everyone in Angowrie would be thinking the same way: that we were all in this together. Like when the seniors won the premiership in the District League and the whole town celebrated. Or Carols by Candlelight on the riverbank every Christmas, when you'd look around and see your mates with their families, their faces all lit by the glow of their small flames.

But that day outside the supermarket, everything changed.

It was a warm day in autumn, about three months after news of the first outbreak. Fresh food was getting scarce and people were starting to avoid going out in public. But that morning there was a crowd milling about and hassling Jim Sackville to open the supermarket and let people get the food they needed.

They weren't talking about paying for it, though. It was a strange sight, everyone with their white masks on, trying not to breathe too close to anyone else but still forming a mob.

Jim panicked, pointed his shotgun to the sky and pulled the trigger. The blast ripped through the air and everyone fell quiet. Then I heard a voice I knew—Dad's. He was standing next to Jim with his hands in the air. He pulled his mask down to speak.

'All right, everyone,' he said. 'Let's just keep calm. Jim's got a right to guard his business. This is his livelihood.'

A bloke named Scully, who I recognised from the football club, stepped forward. He had a ratty sort of face with a long, thin nose and his voice sounded weaselly through his mask. As he spoke he kept looking over his shoulder for support from the crowd, but most of them were still making up their mind about what to do.

'It's gone past that stage, mate,' he said to Dad. 'We're running out of food and none of us have got any money to buy it. We gotta help each other now.'

From the other side of the crowd I could see Dad talking quietly with Jim, who listened but then shook his head and raised the shotgun again, this time aiming it at Scully. The last thing I saw was Dad reaching over to grab the barrels.

It went off, maybe accidentally, I don't know, but someone in the front of the crowd must have been hit because there was yelling and screaming and everyone pushed forward, trapping Jim and Dad against the locked doors of the supermarket. I heard the sound of breaking glass, and when I got a clear view again the doors had given way and the crowd had pushed through into the shop. They clawed and jumped over each other to get to the shelves. Some groups worked together, grabbing trolleys and running down the aisles, shovelling food off the shelves with long sweeps of their arms.

I elbowed my way through to find Dad. I saw him off to the side of the entrance near the check-out, kneeling over Jim and pushing up and down on his chest. There was blood all over the floor. Eventually Dad's hands slowed and he slumped against the wall.

People were fighting each other for food, punching and kicking anyone out of their way. I saw my old football coach, George Wilson, barge his way down an aisle. He caught my eye and shrugged his shoulders, as if to say, *What else is there to do?* I realised I knew most of the looters—and that's when I understood that there'd be no going back from here.

When I glanced at Dad his eyes were closed, and I saw that he was bleeding. He had a huge gash up high on his thigh and he'd put his hand there to stop it spurting.

I shook him by the shoulders and his eyes opened.

'Come on, Dad. We've got to get out of here.'

He struggled to his feet and we stumbled out through the doors just as a ute backed up onto the footpath and crashed though the main display window of the bottle shop. Men inside started loading cartons of beer straight from the fridge.

I don't know how we made it home, but Mum ran out to meet us as we came around the corner. Dad was really weak by this stage, hardly able to stand up and mumbling stuff I couldn't understand. He fell into Mum's arms and the three of us toppled to the ground.

Sometimes I go and visit the spot where Dad fell, back near our old house. I can still remember every detail of that day. How I was trapped under his weight and I couldn't shift him. How Mum had taken her shirt off and wrapped it tight around his leg, but the blood just kept coming. She was crying and pushing her face up against his, telling him to hold on, telling him how much we needed him.

Everything seemed to go still then. Mum's arm came around and held my shoulder. I looked up to see her lying next to him. She knew before I did what was going to happen. So we lay there on the side of the road, the three of us together, wound around each other and holding on like some great force was trying to tear us apart. The pounding in my ear, the big heart in his big chest, began to slow down and the spaces between beats grew longer. I held Dad tight and Mum took his face in her hands, kissing him on his lips. She held him like that until the cold of the evening dropped on us and I couldn't hear his heart anymore.

With the light all but gone now, it's safe to get the fire going in the lounge. The moon is hidden behind thick cloud, so even if the town is being watched from up on the ridge the smoke won't be visible.

I've got two rabbits to boil up. We'll eat one tonight and keep one for tomorrow.

When the next storm front hits, the house rattles and shakes. Rowdy is restless, whimpering and whining with the thunder and lightning, pushing himself against my legs and burying his nose in my jumper. I pull him in close and we both huddle under a blanket in front of the fire. This calms him down and before long he's snoozing in my lap. Just the sound of him breathing is comforting.

After that day at the supermarket, the whole town began to fall apart. Locals started ransacking houses looking for food, fuel and medicine. In the weeks before he died, Dad had been stockpiling stuff from his hardware store in an old garage at the back of a property on a quiet street away from the middle of town. He only knew about it because he used to deliver gas bottles to the holiday house next door, but it meant we had our own supplies.

The virus was spreading faster. Angowrie was quarantined, with no one allowed in or out, but most people were too scared to stick around. They took off into the bush to find their way north, carrying whatever they could in handcarts and pushers. There was hardly any fuel left, either. A group of men had taken over the petrol station, guarding it night and day. When the electricity dropped out they set up hand pumps to bleed the tanks into forty-four-gallon drums that they traded for food.

In the end, I still don't know how many people died and how many left, but pretty soon the town was close to deserted. Mum and I sat up into the night and tried to decide what would be best—to try our luck going north or to stick it out in Angowrie and hope that things got better? As much as we talked I reckon we both knew we wouldn't leave. We had buried Dad in the backyard, and neither of us could bring ourselves to leave him.

Then Mum got sick.

Rowdy and me had come back from setting our traps one afternoon and heard the coughing from inside the house. Mum yelled at me through the window not to come in, to stay outside.

I opened the back door slowly and saw her sitting at the kitchen table, and it hit me then how tired she had been those past few days, going to bed early and getting up later each morning. She looked up at me and held up a hand.

'*No, Finn. Stop,*' she cried. 'You can't come in. Don't come near me.'

I stood, frozen, in the doorway. Her hair and clothes were wet with perspiration, and her whole body was shaking.

'Listen to me, darling, listen carefully. Go and sleep in the house next to the storage shed with all our supplies. I'll be okay. Don't worry about me. I love you, Finny. You know that, don't you? I love you with all my heart and there's nothing I want to do more right now than hug you. But you can't come back here, baby. Never. You understand? Never.'

Now, when I think about that day, I struggle to picture her face. It's strange the things that stay with me, standing there and looking at my mum for the last time. I remember the light, the way the sun slanted through the kitchen window and caught the wall. I remember the smell of the rabbit I was holding and the feel of the rough pads on the bottom of its feet. And I remember the way Rowdy hung back from the door like he could sense the disease.

I went out to our shed and lay down on an old mattress on the floor. I slept on and off, hugging Rowdy to keep warm. In the morning the house was quiet, but the back door was open and I could see right through the kitchen and down the hallway. Even though I knew it was dangerous, I walked down to Mum's bedroom.

Her bed was empty and the sheets cold. She was gone.

I spent most of that day searching for her. I tried to get Rowdy to track her, but he backed away when I held a shirt of Mum's under his nose.

I took my bike and ventured further out onto the tracks that led north. She wouldn't have been able to walk far.

By the time the sun had set and the light dropped away I was up the top of the valley near the fences. I'd stopped crying; I don't think I had any more tears in me.

I found myself in my favourite spot, on top of the ridge overlooking the whole town. With no lights, no movement, no humans, it was just the shell of a town really—maybe not a town at all, just burned-out shops and ransacked houses.

A few months after I lost Mum, I discovered Ray. I had been hunting out in the Addiscot Valley, about two hours east of town. As I was setting traps along a fence line, I looked up to see this old bloke pointing a shotgun at me from about twenty metres away.

'Oi,' he said. 'Bugger off.'

I was so shocked to hear another voice I just stood there staring at him.

'Go on,' he said, 'I told you to bugger off my land.' He jerked the shotgun at the bush behind me.

'Sorry,' I said. 'Just trying to catch some food.'

He lowered the gun and turned his head to the side like he was hard of hearing.

'I know you, don't I?' he said.

I couldn't place him. His hair was long and wild and grey, and most of his face was hidden behind a beard.

'You're Tom Morrison's boy, aren't you? From the hardware?'

'Yeah.'

'You always spoke funny,' he said, scratching his chin. 'I

recognise your dog, too.'

'Rowdy.'

'Yeah, well,' he said. 'I'm sorry, son, but I only got enough food for myself. How you faring?'

'Getting by. Mostly rabbits and fish.'

'Your mum and dad?'

'Both gone.'

'How long you been on your own?'

I shrugged. 'Maybe six months.'

He was nodding and looking past me into bush, as though he was expecting someone else to be with me.

'Seen any Wilders about?'

This was the first time I'd heard about the gangs of men roaming the country to the north.

'Nope,' I said.

'Many people left in town?'

'None. Just Rowdy and me.'

'None?'

'Yep.'

'Shit.'

Through that first winter me and Ray traded food every month or so. I'd catch rabbits for him and he'd give me honey from his hives or veggies grown in his garden. It was tempting to move out there and live with him—I reckon he would have liked that—but I had my stores to protect and his farm was too far from the surf.

This storm is taking its time to clear. I don't sleep well, worrying about how the house will stand up to the rain and wind.

The next day, when I check the river mouth in the afternoon, the sets are lining up like corduroy. Dad used to say that; meant they were one after the other. So I grab my board and paddle out again, duck diving under the sets as they crash over the bar. They're bigger today and I need to be careful not to drift too far inside the peak.

But I've only had a couple of waves when I hear Rowdy going apeshit. When I look back to the beach I can hardly believe what I see. He's got someone bailed up, leaping up and down and barking at them, then dropping to the ground like he's ready to go at them. I'm whistling for him to back off, but the waves are making too much noise for him to hear me. *There's nothing for it*, I end up thinking. *I'll have to head in.*

I undo my leg-rope in the shallows and hold the board in front of me in case I need protection. But this bloke's just standing there, putting his hand out, trying to soothe Rowdy.

When I get closer I see he's as small as me, thin as a whippet. Rangy. Hair long and ropey right down his back and falling across his face. He's wearing an old pair of shorts and a way too big jumper.

Then he starts talking and it hits me. It's a girl. Voice real high and panicky.

'You gotta help me,' she says. 'Wilders. They're coming. They're tracking me.'

2

I'm struck dumb like an idiot. I haven't heard a girl's voice in so long it takes time to sink in. I understand enough to sense danger, though.

I drop my board and take off for the safety of the tea trees. She's onto the idea now and so is Rowdy, all three of us belting up the dunes, sending sand flying in the air behind us.

We reach the top and dive under the overhang. The girl's got me by the arm and she's not letting go. I peer out and see five of them—Wilders. I've steered clear of gangs like this when I've come across them north of the fence lines. As far as I know they haven't ventured into town before.

These are big blokes. No guns, but carrying long bits of wood. Looks like knives taped to the ends. It's no secret which way we've taken off, with our tracks all the way up the dune like a big sign saying, 'Up here, up here'.

I see them start to climb, lumbering-like. Slow. And not real smart, either. They don't split up and try to head us off. Like dogs on the scent of a feed, all running together in a pack. I know I've got them covered but I don't get cocky. I've always had a plan for this. Head for the bush upriver. Lead them away from home. Get into the thick mimosa and stay low, then double back home after dark.

She's still got me by the arm, the girl, hanging on like a leech. Even in the panic I think how strange it feels to have someone touching me. So I look at her and say, 'Keep up,' and start running again.

Rowdy bolts ahead like it's a big game, and the girl's matching me stride for stride, doing it easy by the looks. We've got a hundred metres on them by the time they fight their way out into the open. I slow a bit because I want them to see us. I've got to draw them away from home. I hear them yelling and hollering, probably thinking they're onto us.

I reckon we've got them beat when I hear it. It takes a while to sink through my thick head because I haven't heard that noise in so long it's like an echo. A motor. I look up and there's another big bastard on a trailbike weaving his way through the tussock grass and coming straight for us. He's got a metal stake in his hand and he's holding it like it's a tennis racquet.

We're running out of options. I don't think we'll make it to the mudflats. I look to the girl, her eyes wide, and I say one thing.

'Swim.'

I run to the bank of the river and wade out into the current. She's beside me and Rowdy's next to her. The tide's coming in so as soon as we get into deep water it starts to sweep us along. We keep stroking hard so we can get to the other bank well short of the bridge.

The girl swims like a mullet. She's climbing the bank by the time I get there and reaching down to me. She's streaming wet, all her clothes sticking to her bones and she's looking at me kind of fierce and needy at the same time. I take her hand and it's strong.

The Wilders are jumping up and down on the other side like they've never seen a river before. Rowdy clambers up the bank and shakes himself dry. No time for resting, though, and we take off into the scrub, heading for the hills.

I lead us up to the ridge above the football ground where I stop and look back down to the river, watching and working out what they're going to do. Eventually they walk towards the road bridge, the trailbike moving ahead of the pack.

They cross slowly, maybe wary of being ambushed. It doesn't look as though they're going to track us right away. The trailbike circles back to them and they spend a long time standing around and pointing up towards the ridge.

The sun's getting low by the time they give up, lazy bastards, and I see them heading north towards the fences, where I'm guessing they came from.

The girl's staring at me now, backing away.

'What's your name?' she says, out of breath. She has an accent I've never heard before.

'Fnn,' I say, and the name sounds funny. I haven't said it in so long.

'Finn?' she says, stretching the *i* sound out.

'Yeah.'

'Why do you speak like that?'

'Like what?' I say.

'Growly.'

There's no time to explain now.

The sun's gone when I get to my feet. I wait for a bit to see what she's going to do before I start walking home.

I hear her following me, kind of stop-start like she's not sure. Rowdy's padding along next to her as though he's known her all his life.

'I'm Rose,' she says at last.

There are words running around inside my head, but I can't get them to come out right. So I don't say anything. I just turn round to look at her. She's maybe eighteen or nineteen, though it's hard to tell because her black hair is so long and wild and her clothes are too big for her. Her skin is dark, like she might be Indian, and her arms and legs are covered in cuts and scratches and scars. She's got a rag tied around one hand with blood seeping through it.

It's a stand-off. Her hair keeps falling over her face, but her eyes are sharp like knives.

'You live here?' she asks.

'Maybe. Where d'you come from?'

I can see her trying to figure out what I'm saying, piecing the words together. 'North,' she says.

'Wilder country?'

She nods.

'You a Wilder?'

'Do I look like a Wilder to you? I escaped from them and I'm never going back.'

The night is closing in. Even though I've still got my wetsuit on, the wind is cutting through me. She's shivering too. I make a sign for her to follow me down the track towards town.

A strange sort of silence comes over us. I'm trying to put together everything that's happened since I paddled out for my surf. I've made decisions without having time to think them through. The last two winters I've had nothing but time, but today everything has changed in a couple of hours.

I can hear Rose behind me as we make our way down from the ridge. I'm still wary of the Wilders being about, tricking us into leading them to my place, so I take a roundabout route, scouting along the banks of the river, keeping low until we get to the flats by the mouth.

We're lying in the tussock grass when she crawls up next to me, almost on top of me. Close up, she looks like she's been living rough. There are little bits of twigs and leaves caught in her hair. And the smell of her.

It's something I'd almost forgotten about, the smell people have. I could always tell when Mum had been in a room just by the smell she left behind. It must have been the deodorant she used, or the perfume, and I loved its sweetness and the way it seemed to just hang in the air. Dad too, though he was different. There was linseed oil from all the old furniture he used to work on in the shed. And two-stroke. The smells from the hardware: rope and paint and fertiliser. Somehow he seemed to carry all of them around with him.

And now here's this girl, Rose, and she stinks like piss and sweat, a bit like the smell of the melaleucas after it's been raining for a few days and the leaves on the ground start to rot.

'What'd you think?' she says, pointing to the river mouth.

In my mind I'm trying out the words before I say them.

'They could be trying to trick us,' I say. I clear my throat and try some more. 'Could have doubled back on their tracks, watching for us.'

I'm on a roll now, like I'm discovering a new language and I can't use enough of it.

'I reckon we wait till it gets darker and then cross at the mouth. The tide's turned so we should be able to wade across. We'll be out in the open, though.'

She has this unnerving way of looking straight at me while I'm talking. I figure she's trying to read my lips.

'I don't know what you just said, but if you can point to where we're going, that'd be good,' she says. Again, there's the accent I can't place. It's sort of singsong, like she rolls the words over on top of each other.

I point to the other side of the river. 'My place is back up the hill, on the other side of town. Once we get over the river we'll be sweet. There's lots of cover.'

'Okay.' She nods. 'We have to cross the river and go up the hill. So we wait till it gets darker.'

She makes it sound like it's her idea.

She turns onto her back then and buries herself down in the tussocks. We're up above the high-tide mark so the sand is dry and soft.

'Thanks,' she says. 'For helping me.'

'Didn't have much choice, did I?'

It sounds harder than I mean it to.

'I mean,' I say, 'not with the Wilders and all. Bastards, that lot.'

She turns to me and I see how dark her eyes are. Dark and shaped like almonds.

She doesn't hold my gaze, staring down at the sand like she's embarrassed. We lie like this for ages, until a quarter-moon begins to rise. Rowdy has been watching the whole thing and he seems confused, looking to me then to Rose. He starts to lick the salt off my feet.

'Time to go,' I say, finally. 'We'll get some cover on the other side of the dune until we get down to the mouth. We've got no choice then, out into the open. We'll have to run to get to the water. Stick together. Signal. No talking.'

There's no movement on the other side of the river and the sand under our feet means we can move quietly. Finally we get to the beach and start our run to the water. The tide's slacker now, but there's still a strong pull. I feel Rose take my hand and together we wade across.

Rowdy is ahead of us, already on the other bank. He knows

there's something up and that he needs to keep quiet. Just as it starts to get shallower, and we think we're in the clear, a noise erupts behind us. In the weak moonlight I can see half-a-dozen figures silhouetted along the top of the dune.

'Warda,' a man's voice yells and it sounds like pain and anger mixed in together. '*Warda!*'

Rose grabs my arm so tight her fingernails dig into my skin. She doesn't stop moving, doesn't turn around—just pulls us both up onto the bank, lets go of my arm and starts running for cover. I come after her and find her crouched under the first line of tea trees.

The screaming from the other bank hasn't let up, but the noise of the waves and wind in the trees drown out the words until it sounds like a dog howling.

Rose squats on her haunches and her whole body seems to be heaving with the effort to breathe. I can hear the snot in her nose with each inhale.

'Don't let them get me. I can't go back,' she says. Her voice cracks.

We have to move. I find the way to the track that takes us under the old viewing platform and away to safety on the hill overlooking the river.

It's not until we are getting closer to my place that doubt starts to creep in. I've been living here on my own for so long it's like I'm about to break something sacred, something that's just been about Rowdy and me. We've guarded it, protected it, hidden it away. It's our secret and now I'm going to share it with someone I've only known for a couple of hours. How do I know I can trust her? How do I know she's not in with the Wilders and waiting to lead them here when she finds out where we live? I slow my pace.

She knows what's going on straightaway. 'You can blindfold me if you want to,' she says.

I can barely see her in the dark now and a thought comes into my head: *I could leave her here*. It'd be easy. But there's a stronger feeling that makes up my mind for me. It comes from what she said back there under the tea trees—how angry and how deep it was.

'No, it's okay,' I say. 'Just follow close.'

We cut through the houses to climb the hill for couple of blocks, then trace the line of sheoaks that drop their needles like a carpet until we come out by my back shed. I hold up my hand and peer around the corner at the house. Everything is quiet.

'Clear,' I whisper and we walk across the yard. Rowdy brushes past and goes straight to his blanket in the corner. I know my way around the house without even thinking, but she'll be unfamiliar with everything.

I grab one of the kitchen chairs and ease her into it. On top of the mantelpiece I find the torch and switch it on. She starts at the sudden light.

'You've got light,' she says. 'Batteries!'

I keep the beam pointed at the floor.

'My dad owned the hardware before…you know, before.'

In the glow of the torch I can see her nod.

'Look around,' I say. 'Get your bearings. I can't afford to

leave the torch on for long. The batteries are precious.'

She follows the beam around the kitchen. It's strange looking at it like this, breaking up something I know so well into small parts for her to take in—the sink, the fridge with its pilot light glowing soft down by the floor, the table and chairs. I realise I have never moved any of the other chairs out even though there's only ever been me here; like I've been waiting for someone else to turn up.

'A fridge!' she says, a little too loud.

'Gas. I'll explain later.'

She squats down on the floor and reaches her hand to the pilot light like it might not be real.

'Come with me,' I say.

I show her the lounge room, the bedrooms, the bathroom. 'Tank water,' I say, before she asks. 'Had a wet spring so plenty at the moment.'

Back in the kitchen we sit down and I turn off the torch. The darkness swamps us again until my eyes adjust and I make out the shapes I'm used to. I open the fridge and take out the rabbit I cooked last night.

Somehow, it's easier talking to her in the dark.

'The fridge?' she asks.

'Gas bottles,' I say. 'When everything was falling apart, Dad and me moved a heap of them into sheds around town. I know where they all are. Won't last for ever, but at least I've got fuel for now.'

There's a long silence then with just the sound of me cracking the bones of the rabbit as I pull it apart. I find a plate on the sink and put the meat on it. The gamey smell fills the kitchen.

I move around, pulling down all the blinds and shutting the doors, like I've done so many times on my own. I want to see her now, so I light the candle I keep on the side bench. She looks different in its glow, softer. I can't see her cuts and scrapes and scars.

'Hungry?' I ask.

Without taking the time to answer she grabs a piece of rabbit and pushes it into her mouth, chewing and breathing hard. Then she takes another piece, and another.

'Easy,' I say.

I take a piece of meat before it's all gone. She gnaws on the bones, breaking them open and sucking the marrow out.

'Sorry,' she says. 'I haven't eaten cooked food in a while.' Her eyes are still darting around the room, like there might be danger lurking somewhere.

'That's okay.' I take what's left of the rabbit and give it to Rowdy.

When I look back Rose has slumped over her arms, her head turned sideways and, as best I can tell, her eyes are closed. I tap her shoulder and she reels back in her chair.

'Down the hall,' I say, pointing. 'Bedroom on the right.'

'Okay,' she says. 'Thanks. But tell me, what's with the growly voice?'

I'm kind of relieved to get it out of the way.

'I had trouble talking when I was little. Something to do with the muscles in my mouth. I guess the last couple of years on my own haven't helped.'

She doesn't say anything, just nods, gets to her feet and backs away down the hallway. I hear the bedroom door close.

I sit at the table a little while longer, trying to figure whether it's a good or a bad thing that she's shown up. She's brought the Wilders into town—that'll be a problem. I'll have to be more careful. No surfing for a while. And I'll have to take care going out to check the traps.

She has thrown up a whole new set of problems to deal with. But something else is sitting at the back of my mind too, something that knows how good it feels to have someone here with me, someone to take the edge off the loneliness. But she's so wary of everything, I can't even be sure she'll stay.

Something else's nagging at me—the name the Wilder called out from the other side of the river. I heard it loud and clear. *Warda*. I'll ask her about it in the morning.

Later, as I lie in bed, I listen for the familiar sounds of the house, the wind in the big cypress at the side, the ends of the branches rubbing against the spouting, Rowdy snorting and farting and changing position on his blanket. There is something new in the feel of the place now that the girl is here. I can't even bring myself to say her name out loud yet, but in the dark I roll it around on my tongue. *Rose*. It has a round feel to it and I have to make a circle with my lips to get the *o* sound. First just a whisper, all breath. I move the sound further up, away from my throat and it starts to take on the shape of her name.

Rose.

3

When I get up in the morning she's already sitting at the kitchen table. There are thick scabs on her elbows and a deep, recent cut on the back of her left hand. And there is still the smell of her, sweet and tart at the same time.

'Hey,' I say. 'How'd you sleep?'

'Sleep? Yeah, good. First time in a bed for ages. You?'

'Okay. Got up a couple of times just to keep watch. No sign of them, though.'

'We're safe here, yeah?'

'Yeah, safe enough. We're at the back of another property. You can't see it from the road at the front and I've blocked the drive with tea tree. It's only noise or smoke that can give us away.'

I remind myself to slow down when I'm talking with her.

'That cut doesn't look good,' I say.

She lays her hand palm-down on the tabletop. The wound is deep and the skin around it is red and puffy. It runs diagonally across the back of her hand and is about four centimetres long.

'How'd it happen?'

'Doesn't matter,' she says. 'You got anything we can put on it?'

I don't press her, heading to the bathroom to get the tube of antiseptic cream I've used a couple of times when I've cut myself on the rocks diving for abalone. I grab some cotton buds too.

I settle myself back at the table opposite her and turn her hand around in the light. She winces.

'It's deep,' I say. 'Was it a knife?'

She snatches her hand back. 'It's just a cut, all right,' she says. 'I caught it on a branch.'

I must have completely forgotten how to talk to people without them getting angry. Everything I say seems to be wrong. The whole place is quiet except for Rowdy's snuffling in the corner. I'm looking at the table and fiddling with the tube of antiseptic.

She sits on the edge of her chair and places her hand on the table again. Her back is arched and her leg is jigging up and down.

'You should clean it,' I say.

I get a stainless steel bowl from the cupboard below the sink. I half fill it with water, pour in a little salt and sit back down, pushing the bowl to her side of the table. It's like approaching a wounded animal.

She eases her hand into the bowl and starts dabbing at the wound with a wet cotton bud. When she looks up her eyes bore through me, hard and sharp again.

She braces her body against the pain, but digs right into the middle of the cut, reopening it so that puss and blood start to seep into the water.

It's worse than I thought. 'It needs stitches,' I say.

'You reckon?'

'I've got Mum's sewing kit.'

'Just get me the thinnest needle you can find and some strong thread.'

I bring the whole sewing box and she rustles through it, finally picking a needle and some red thread.

'Sorry,' she says, 'but I'm going to have to use some gas to boil the water. We need to sterilise the needle.'

I'm grateful to have something to do. Seeing Rose at the table with the sewing kit, I can't help but think of Mum. She used to sit up in the kitchen in our old place, darning socks and repairing holes in clothes. She'd have this lamp on the table and her hands would work away under the light. I can see her there, letting down my winter school pants and joking that I'd need to stop growing soon.

A few minutes later, I'm fishing the needle out of the boiling water with a pair of tongs and placing it on the table.

'Now,' Rose says, 'I need your help.'

She threads the needle, takes a deep breath and pierces the

little ridge I make by pushing the sides of the wound together. I hear the sharp intake of breath as the thread catches, but she keeps pulling. She loops it back and through half-a-dozen times before she ties it off and holds up the thread for me to cut with the scissors.

As soon as I do this she lurches away from the table, opens the back door and spews over the rail. But before I can even get up, she's walked back into the kitchen wiping her mouth with her good hand. She fills a glass with water, gargles and spits it back into the sink.

She sits down, lays her hand on the table and says, 'Better get that antiseptic onto it, I reckon.'

I dab the line of stitches with the cream.

'You're a good sewer,' I say.

'I'm a shit sewer,' she says, but there's no hardness in her voice. 'Never saw the point of it. Wish I'd learned better now, though.'

I find a bandage in the bathroom cabinet and hold her wrist while I wrap it around the wound and fasten it with a clip.

'You'll need to clean it every day and make sure the infection doesn't spread.'

'Thanks, Mum,' she says, and for the first time I see how white and even her teeth are when she smiles.

For a minute we just sit there looking at each other. It's so much easier when you've got something to do. I get the sense she's weighing me up again.

'How long you been on your own here?' she asks.

'Not sure. Since everyone else left. After the quarantine.

After all the phones went down and the shops were emptied out. Maybe two years. Could be longer. Where'd you come from?'

'We lived on a farm out past Longley. We'—she pauses and takes a breath—'Stan and Beth and my sister Kas.'

'Where are they now?'

She hesitates, looking past me to the open window. 'Kas is out there somewhere. We got separated a couple of days back. It makes me sick to think what might've happened to her.'

'And Stan and Beth? Are they your mum and dad?'

She pauses then and looks straight at me. 'Kas and me are Sileys. Stan and Beth, they were our owners.'

I know about Sileys. Asylum seekers. Mum used to talk about them all the time, and they were on the news a lot. The government ran offshore camps for years, detention centres. At some stage they decided to bring the young, fit Sileys to the mainland to work. Refugee reassignment, they called it. Mum called it slavery.

'Were you factory workers?'

Rose's voice is calm, tired, like she's had to explain this before.

'Some went to factories. Doing every shitty job they couldn't get locals to do. Abattoirs. Sewage works. Chicken factories. Kas and me, we were lucky. We got to breathe fresh air every day. And Stan and Beth were okay. They came to the auction at the processing centre and bought us. We were so relieved. There were people looking for young girls to buy.'

'How old were you?'

'Twelve. Kas was nine.'

She pauses then and picks at the bandage on her hand.

'Stan and Beth had no kids of their own. They taught us to read and speak English, gave us time off, even took us into Longley to go shopping.'

I'm looking at the darkness of her skin, the deep brown of her eyes.

'So where are you from? What country?'

'Afghanistan. I don't remember much about home, though. We lived in a camp in Pakistan for years before...'

'Before what?'

'Mum and Dad, they sold everything they had so Kas and me could get to Indonesia. We went with an uncle they trusted.'

'Where are your parents now?'

Her head drops.

'I haven't seen them since I left the camp in Peshawar. This is all I have to remember them,' she says, reaching inside her jumper and pulling out a gold ring attached to a strip of leather looped around her neck.

'And you've got no idea where Kas is?'

'No.' She hugs her arms to her chest and rocks back and forth. 'We lost each other on the way to the coast.'

I still can't get a handle on her story, how it all fits together.

'So you and Kas were sold to Stan and Beth? What happened after that?'

'Their farm was west of Longley. We lived there for about five years, until the virus came. We thought we'd be okay. We were used to killing our own stock and growing food. We had milk, eggs, and Stan grew spuds. But after a couple of months people started coming out from Longley, turning up at the gate and asking for food. Wasn't long before they stopped asking. There were people on the road. I don't blame them—everyone was hungry. But they brought the disease. You know about the women?'

'Yeah, it was the same here.'

For some reason the virus affected women more than men. One of the last bulletins we heard before the internet went down said ten women were dying for every one male.

Rose sighs. 'Beth, she was all for helping people, but it meant she talked to them, touched them. Stan would get so angry with her about it. I don't know why, but she wasn't affected. Once Stan was killed...'

She gets up from the table and walks over to the window above the sink. I hardly hear what she says next, it's so close to a whisper.

'After that it was just Beth and me and Kas.'

I don't know what to say. For ages I've only thought about what's happened to me, the people I've lost, what I've needed to do to survive. I haven't had time to think about anyone else or what they might have been through. And she said Stan was *killed*. She didn't say he *died*. Before I can ask her about him, though, she pulls herself together and comes back to the table.

'We thought we'd be safer on the farm. You remember all the rumours about people starting to panic, huge queues for petrol and food?'

I nod. 'We thought we'd be safe down here, too.'

'Stan had started to stockpile grain in an old tank. And

seed potatoes in the barn. But he wanted more. So he went into town...'

She stops then and leans forward so the hair falls over her face. She does that thing I'm getting used to—flinging her head back and pulling the hair behind her ears.

'Secretly, me and Kas didn't believe that things were as bad as Stan and Beth were making out,' she continues. 'We thought the government would get on top of it, someone would find a vaccine in time. We just had to hold out for a while until things got back to normal.'

'Same here. We kept expecting to see the Red Cross or the army come rolling into town, telling us everything was okay.'

Rose has taken the leather strap from around her neck and looped it over her wrist. She slides a finger in and out of the ring.

'When Stan didn't come home Kas and I weren't worried. He was good friends with Mr Kincaid, the auctioneer at the sale yards, and he'd sometimes stay with him instead of driving back in the dark.

'The next morning was so quiet. I realised there was no sound of cars or trucks out on the highway. There hadn't been mail deliveries for weeks and none of the neighbours stopped by anymore. When Kas and me came into the kitchen for breakfast, Beth had the rifles out on the table and packets of ammo next to them. I couldn't believe it. She never touched the guns. Stan used them to shoot sick animals, but otherwise they stayed locked up in the tractor shed. Now Beth was checking them over! She said we had to be prepared.

'Stan didn't come back that day or the next. By then we

were real worried. So we moved bales around in the hayshed to make a space in the middle and we loaded it up with food and blankets and one of the rifles. Beth said if anyone came Kas and I should run straight out there and stay hidden until she gave the all clear.'

Rose has launched right into this story like she's been waiting to tell it. I want to pull her up, ask more questions, but she doesn't give me the chance.

'Then finally, on Christmas Eve, Stan's ute crawled up the drive. Beth was suspicious so she sent Kas and me out to our hiding spot in the hayshed, just in case. But I couldn't help myself. I climbed up and peeked through a join in the shed wall.

'The ute came up the side of the house and into the yard. I knew for sure then that it wasn't Stan. I had a horrible feeling in my gut. Two men got out and looked around the yard. I couldn't see Beth anywhere but I knew she'd be watching from the house.

'It was a guy called Ramage, and his son, who everyone called Rat.'

There's something in the way she says Ramage's name that hurts her. She's picking at the bandage on her hand again and her voice hardens.

'Ramage used to run the feedstore in Longley. Stan knew him, trusted him, but he was one of those guys you always thought was watching you, especially the girls. He was a creep.'

She pinches her bottom lip between her teeth, weighing me up.

'That was Ramage, the one on the trailbike yesterday.'

I remember the man yelling across the river mouth.

'What was the name he was calling?'

'Warda,' she says. 'That's my Siley name. Ramage always used it. It's Pashto. It means Rose.'

'What happened after they arrived at the farm?' I ask.

Rose sits back in her chair and crosses her arms.

'I got the rifle, loaded it quietly and climbed back up. I could hear Beth's voice. She was standing on the back porch with a rifle in her hands. The men were about twenty metres away from her.

'Ramage did all the talking, saying, "You here all on your own, Mrs Morgan, or you got them pretty Sileys of yours hidin' somewhere?"

'Beth raised the rifle higher and said, "Where's my husband?"

'Ramage said Stan had sent them out here to pick us up. That he'd had an accident in town. Broken his arm.

'I could see Beth didn't believe him. So she says, "Maybe I'll keep the ute and you two can walk back into town. Since it's my husband's."

'From behind I saw Rat looking like he was slouching back into the seat of the ute. But through the open driver's side door I saw him slipping a hand down to pick up something off the floor.

'Now Ramage was moving towards Beth. "Come on," he says, "let's put that gun away and talk sensible, you and me. Things are different now. We need to look after each other, those of us that's left."

'Rat had picked up a metal wheel brace and was sliding it into the belt at the back of his pants, real slow. He stood up and started circling around to Beth's side.

'Ramage was still talking, all confident now. "Come on Mrs Morgan," he says. "You can't shoot us both. Why don't you put that gun down and we'll all go inside and have a nice cup of tea."

'I was so nervous and sweaty I could hardly hold the rifle. But I stood up and opened the door we used to winch the bales through. I braced my feet on the ledge and got Rat in the sights. I don't even know if I meant to squeeze the trigger but suddenly there was a loud bang and Rat collapsed on the ground screaming and grabbing at his leg. At the same time Beth pointed her rifle straight at Ramage, who was looking over at Rat and trying to figure out what had happened.

'"Get off my fucking land," Beth yelled. She never swore. Never.

'She had her rifle pointed at his head now and she said, "Get your mate into the back of the ute. Now!"

'Rat was rolling around on the ground, screaming. I wanted to shoot him again, just to shut him up. But Ramage dragged him to the side of the ute and rolled him into the back. Then Beth called out to me.

'I stood up in the doorway so Ramage could see me pointing the rifle at him. Beth called to Kas to get the cable ties from the shed.

'Then Beth tied one around Ramage's wrists and pushed him down so he was lying next to Rat. There was all this blood in the bottom of the tray.

"I'll be back for you girls," Ramage screamed as Beth was about to climb in the ute. "I know where you are. You can't hide. There'll be more of us next time. We already got the old man."

Rose smiles and shakes her head.

'But then, I'll never forget it: Beth jammed the barrel of the rifle in his mouth. I'd seen her angry before, but nothing like this. It was like something inside her had snapped.

'"You come near my girls," she said, "and I will kill you. You understand, you fucking creep. I will kill you."

'I'm pretty sure I heard his teeth break when she snapped the barrel out of his mouth and got back in the driver's seat. He was bawling now, saying all sorts of dirty things. Things he'd do to Kas and me.

'After Beth took off down the drive it was quiet. Kas and I stood looking at each other. I reckon we both knew nothing was ever going to be normal again.'

'And Beth?' I ask.

Rose takes her time to answer. She shifts in her chair and when she speaks her voice breaks.

'She never came back.'

4

The light is coming right into the kitchen now and my stomach
is rumbling.

'We need to eat,' I say.

I have to make a decision. I always thought if it came to
this, if someone else showed up, I'd have plenty of time to
watch them before I made contact. Check them out. Decide if
I wanted them to see me. But here's Rose right in front of me
and I'm trying to think on my feet. The funny thing is, even
though she's wary, I'm okay with her being here. I can't explain
why exactly. Something about the way she looks, the way she
talks. She's no threat.

'Come with me,' I say.

I ease the back door open and have a good look about. Rowdy slips by my leg for a stretch on the porch.

Rose stands in the doorway. A small shudder passes through her body. Her legs are thin where the shorts fall to her thighs and her feet are bare. She lifts her face to the sun and shades her eyes with her injured hand.

Leading her around the side of the house, I duck through a gap in the old cypress hedge to the garage next door, then pull the branches back and feel under the ledge for the key. I open the door and tell her to follow. It's dark inside, but slowly our eyes adjust.

She stops in the doorway and stares. The garage is lined with shelves full of all sorts of stuff—tinned food, gas bottles, tools, saws, candles, matches, rabbit traps, ropes and nets.

'Wow,' she says. 'Where did you get all this?'

'When things got bad down here, me and Dad started to plan this place. All the shops were cleaned out early on, but we figured there'd be plenty of valuable stuff in the holiday houses.'

'So this is your house, your garage?' she says.

'No. Dad knew everyone left in town would know he owned the hardware and that they'd come to our place before too long. We picked this garage because it looked like it hadn't been used in years and the place next door because it was a holiday house hidden away at the back of the block.'

'Gas,' Rose murmurs, looking at the big cylinders lined up along one wall.

'First thing Dad thought of. He'd just got a big delivery

at the hardware when the town was quarantined.'

'So you can cook food?'

'And run the fridge.'

'Your dad was smart,' she says. She stops then, but I know what she's going to ask.

'He died early on.' I haven't said this out aloud before, that my dad's dead, that I'll never see him again.

'Did you have a mum?'

'She lasted the first winter, but then the virus took her.'

'I'm sorry,' she says.

I start rearranging some tins of beans on a shelf, trying to look busy. It's easier to bury things when you don't have to talk about them with anyone.

'Anyway,' I say, 'let's get some breakfast.'

After I've grabbed a couple of cans of beans, I walk back out into the light. Rose follows, but she's looking over her shoulder into the shed like she can't believe what she's seen. I lock up, put the branches back and hide the key.

Back in the kitchen I get started on cooking. I remember I have two eggs in the fridge. There are chooks that have gone wild and a while ago I found their nest.

'Eggs,' she says with excitement in her voice again.

She takes one of them from my hand and sits it in the flat of her palm, still with a look of disbelief on her face at what I've shown her.

I light a match and the stove hisses to life. Before I can put the pan on it, Rose comes over and holds her hands above the flame.

I cook up the eggs and the beans, frying them until they're

just right. When I turn around, Rose has set the table with knives and forks laid out and a glass of water at each place.

'I just had to do that,' she says.

'No worries,' I say.

'Nowrriz,' she says, deep and low, and I realise that's what I sound like to her.

We eat in not-quite silence. I remember how she ate the rabbit last night and that she probably spewed most of that up on the garden. She finishes hers before I'm even halfway through mine, wipes her mouth with the back of her good hand then picks up the plate and licks it clean. She burps loudly.

'Sorry,' she says. 'Beth never allowed us to do that.'

I try to muster a burp of my own but fail miserably.

She laughs, her eyes softening for a few seconds, but then her face grows serious.

'What do we do now, Finn?'

'Well, first I have to go and check my traps. I set them yesterday morning. I don't want to leave them any longer.'

'Traps?'

'For rabbits. That's what you ate last night. Most of it's on the garden now I reckon.'

She smiles.

As I get ready to go out, I have a churning feeling in my gut. I hardly know this girl and I'm leaving her with everything I have. The house, my food, the stores. Everything. But I can't see any way around it right now. She's seen it all already and she could probably find her way back here if she needed to. Or lead someone else back.

Before I leave I bring out the bow and arrows from my room.

'You know how to use these?' I ask, handing them to her.

'Kinda. Aim and shoot, yeah?'

'Close enough. I'll be a couple of hours. I'll give you a whistle like this when I get back,' I say, making a noise like a wattle-bird, 'Don't come out unless you hear it.'

I'm extra cautious today, taking the long way around behind the golf club to get to the ridge. Rowdy sticks close. At the top of the ridge I stop and scan the town below, but there's no sign of movement, nothing to put my nerves more on edge.

I've laid the traps along the old fence line that marks the start of the farmland. Today's a good day. I get three. I stretch their necks quickly and tie some twine around their back legs. Then I reset the traps.

As I'm heading back down into the cover of the bush, something catches my eye; something glinting in the sun across the paddock in an old hayshed.

I duck down and watch, thinking it's just a tin or a bit of glass catching the light. Then it moves.

I place my hand over Rowdy's muzzle. He knows what this means and drops his belly to the ground. I'm too low down to make out what it is so I crawl along to a low-slung stringybark and shimmy up into the branches. I'm holding my breath, but I can feel my heart pounding against the bark of the tree.

There are at least half-a-dozen men sitting around a fire. Up higher, I catch the smell of meat cooking. I'm not sure they're the Wilders that chased us yesterday until I see the trailbike catching the morning sun. There are blankets strewn across the hay bales and I can see two large red containers.

At least I know where Ramage is now and that he's not back in town hunting for Rose. But he could be getting ready to try again too. I'll have to come back up later in the afternoon and check on them.

I drop quietly down out of the tree, gather up the rabbits, touch Rowdy on his collar and we back away into the scrub.

I've been gone a couple of hours by the time I get back to the house. I whistle to Rose and her head bobs up at the kitchen window.

'All good?' I ask as I come through the door. When I see her I stop in my tracks.

'I hope it's all right,' she says.

She has washed. I can smell soap. Her hair is still wet and dripping a little on her shoulders. Her skin is scrubbed almost raw and a few of the smaller cuts are bleeding. A new white bandage covers the wound on the back of her hand. But that's not what I'm looking at. She is wearing Mum's clothes, a blue dress that comes down just below her knees, a big floppy jumper and a pair of sneakers. Her hands are by her sides, clutching the material tight in her fingers.

'I can take them off.'

'No, it's okay. It's just…'

'They were your mum's.'

I nod. 'She liked that dress. Dad always said it suited her. Matched her eyes, or something. I never noticed.'

Different parts of my world are colliding, parts that have no right to meet. There's some stuff that I've buried so deep that I never thought I'd face it again. Mum wearing that dress is one of them.

'I'll take it off, Finn. I'm sorry. I never should have put it on.'

She starts to walk out of the kitchen. I don't know why it happens or even how, but the next thing I know I'm standing behind her and I've got my hand on her shoulder.

'Rose,' I say, and she turns around to look at me because it's the first time I've called her by her name. 'Please, it's okay. I like it.'

Neither of us knows what to say next, so I pick up the rabbits and take them out the back to the wooden bench under the cypress tree. I slit the first one behind the neck and peel the skin all the way back to the hind legs. Then I gut it. I open up the cavity a bit more with the knife and make sure it's cleaned out. It feels good to be doing something without having to think about it.

When I'm done with the three of them, and I've hung the skins out for the maggots to clean, I take the carcasses back into the kitchen and put them in the fridge.

Rose is sitting at the table drying her hair with a towel.

'Good hunting?' she asks.

'Yep. I might make a stew with them.'

'What else have you got that you're not telling me about?'

I can tell from her voice that she wants to make it up to me for wearing Mum's dress without asking.

'Fresh veggies. I've got some growing in a garden up the street. Just tomatoes, zucchini, some onions and stuff.'

'But how?' she asks.

'Seeds. Dad's idea again. We stocked up and now I collect the seeds when the plants die off. And there's Ray.'

'Who's Ray?'

I tell her about meeting Ray back during the first winter.

'I'll take you out to meet him when things quieten down a bit. After the Wilders have moved on.'

I didn't mean to tell her about the hayshed. She's on her feet with the news, pacing up and down.

'How many?' she cries.

'Six that I could see, but there might be more. I saw the trailbike.'

'Ramage!' She spits his name out. 'Did you see anyone else with them?'

'Anyone else? Like who?'

'Kas.'

'I thought you'd been split up?'

She stops pacing and slumps into a chair.

'You need to tell me what's happened, Rose. I need to know what's going on. Whether we're in more danger than I think.'

'There's danger in just being a girl these days, worse still if you're a Siley.'

She sounds more weary than angry. She sighs.

'When Kas and I couldn't defend the farm any longer we tried to get away. There was an old shack up at the far end of the Pennyroyal Valley, so we headed for there. We did pretty well, living off the land mostly, but it didn't last. Ramage's men hunted us down. We tried to run, but it was useless.

'Ramage had this big compound at his feedstore in Longley. High fences, barbed wire along the top. Big gates. Him and his men rounded up all the kids they could find in the district, boys and girls. Most were Sileys, but not all. Some were just kids whose parents had died. There were about fifteen of us. We slept in the hay, with empty chaff bags thrown over us for warmth.'

Her eyes are sharp again, cutting right through me. She swallows hard and continues.

'Ramage hired us out to farmers. We did whatever shitty jobs they wanted done. It was dangerous, especially for the girls. I never let Kas out of my sight. She's only fifteen. I protected her as much as I could. I did some things I'm not proud of.'

She looks at the tabletop, her hair falling over her face again. I wonder if she is going to cry, and all I can think of is how Dad used to be with Mum when she was angry. He'd tell her a joke. Try to get her to smile. I don't think a joke's going to work with Rose.

'You want a cup of tea?' I ask. It sounds all wrong, though, like I haven't been listening to her, or been taking her seriously.

But she surprises me with a laugh and says, 'Thanks,' and the tension drains from the room.

But I haven't thought it through. 'Shit, I haven't got any tea,' I confess, and that makes her really laugh.

'Don't worry about it,' she says as I sit back down. Then

she seems to size me up again.

'Five days ago,' she goes on, 'Kas and I escaped. There was a man, Ken Butler, an old friend of Stan's and a farmer from down near Nelson. He had a big white beard and used to stay with us when the yearling sales were on. He turned up at the feedstore one day and told Ramage he needed two labourers, and that he had food and whisky to trade. He paid more for us than he should've and told Ramage he'd have us back by morning.

'Ken took us across the road to the old hotel. He said he would help us get away from Longley, said we should travel south. There was no guarantee we'd be safe there, but the further away we got from Ramage, the better.

'Kas and I hid in a woodshed behind the hotel until it was dark. It had been cloudy all day, but like a miracle the sky cleared and I could make out the Southern Cross and the Pointers—pointing us south.'

Rose hasn't look at me once during her story. It's like she's reading off the tabletop, her one good hand moving up and down the wood grain, a fingernail pushing into the gap where the boards are joined. She has big hands. The one that's not hidden in the bandage is scabbed all over and her nails are chipped. When she turns it over there are calluses rising up on every joint. Farm girl's hands.

I'm listening to her, but I'm still missing something. I don't know anything about Kas.

'She's my little sister,' Rose explains. 'She always had it tougher than me. She was born with a birthmark on her face,

48

a big red mark that covers one cheek and runs down onto her neck. She could have been embarrassed about it, but it just made her fierce.

'She rode the horses. That was her thing. I was an okay rider, but she was way better. She could talk to them, make them understand her. We used to joke about her being the horse whisperer.'

There's something softer about Rose when she talks about Kas. She narrows her eyes a little, like she can see the shape of her sister but can't quite make out her features.

'After we left Ken, we walked for three days without seeing anyone,' she continues. 'At the end of the third day, we reached a place called Swan's Marsh.'

I nod. 'I know it. On the other side of the main range. We used to play football there sometimes. Did you see anyone there?'

She shakes her head. 'Not at first. We skirted around the back of town, keeping to the trees until we found a safe spot that had a view along the main street. Before I went to check things out, we agreed that, if we got separated, Kas should keep moving towards the coast, as far away from Ramage as possible.'

Rose takes a deep breath.

'I found them out the back of an old general store—four men and a couple of kids sitting around a fire. The smell of cooking meat was driving me wild. I knew it was stupid, but I was so hungry I wasn't thinking straight. I walked out into the open and stood about ten metres from them. They all moved at once, grabbing sticks, and one guy picked up a shovel. They circled me.

'It was so stupid. It was never going to be right for a girl to be travelling on her own unless she was running from someone. A woman stepped out of the back door of the store and came up close to check me out. She had wild red hair and she stank. She smiled—most of her teeth were missing. She said they didn't have much, just a bit of deer they'd shot, but I was welcome to join them.

'So they gave me some food, and I ate like a pig but I didn't care. They all just sat and watched me. Then one of them asked where I was from, and something in his voice gave me the creeps.

'I told them I'd come from the north, that I'd avoided Longley because I'd met people on the road who said bad things about the place. It was weird when I mentioned Longley. One of the men spat into the fire and said they hadn't seen anyone on the road in months. Then he asked me if I was one of Ramage's Sileys.'

Rose looks away and I reckon she's embarrassed. I've got to admit, it sounds pretty dumb to have just walked into danger like that.

'I got to my feet slowly, said thanks and I'd be on my way. But one of them grabbed me, one of the big guys. He tied my hands behind my back and dragged me off to a pump shed at the back of the yard. Said he'd be back for me during the night.'

I have to look away, out the kitchen window to the back-yard. I don't want to hear any more. I don't want to know if she's been abused. But she squares off her shoulders again and stares me down. I know she's going to tell me the rest, even if I don't want to hear it.

'It was pitch black in there,' Rose continues, quieter now, 'and the fumes were making me sick. I must've slept because I woke up when I heard the door opening. I made out a figure in the moonlight and kicked out as hard as I could. Got him in the balls, too.

'He grabbed me by the hair and tried to drag me out of the shed, but then there's this strange sound, like metal hitting bone and the big guy falls sideways onto the pump. Then it goes quiet.'

Rose is shaking her head now, a small smile playing on her lips.

'It was the woman. I couldn't believe it. She helped me up and cut the ropes around my wrists. She started talking fast, telling me I had to run. Ramage would find out eventually and he'd come after me with everything he had. She pushed a chunk of meat into my hands, said us girls have gotta stick together these days. Then I started running.'

The afternoon sun slants through the kitchen window, filling the room with light. Rose turns her face up to the warmth and closes her eyes.

I don't know what to make of her story, but the way she tells it makes me think it's the truth. She talks a lot with her hands, splays them on the table then rakes them back through her hair. And her eyes narrow every now and then when she tries to remember details about what's happened. I'm mesmerised just looking at her, this other person, this *girl,* sitting across from me at the table, her skin, her eyes, her smile that disappears as soon as she lets it sneak out.

'By the time I'd finally made my way back to where I'd left Kas it was getting light. But...' Rose falters. 'She wasn't there. She wasn't *there.* I didn't know what to do. But I couldn't hang around. There was noise coming from down at the general store. I heard shouting. I had to get out of there—fast.

'I was ready to move when something caught my eye at the far end of the street. Someone was moving along at the back of the buildings, staying out of sight but sticking their head out every now and then to check for danger. Someone with long black hair. It was Kas. After a couple of minutes, I saw a horse and rider breaking out across the open paddock. I would have known it was Kas even if I was a mile away, the way her body moved with the horse.

'I'd just started to creep further up the hill when I saw half-a-dozen or so men walking in the open, coming from the north. Ramage's men. They walked straight up to the general store and banged on the door. The woman came out holding a rifle and the men backed off. There was a minute's stand off, and then we all heard the sound of the trailbike. It was coming from the north too, moving real slow and there was a big cloud of dust trailing behind it. It turned up the lane next to the general store...'

Rose looks away. She hides her face behind her hair again and a fat tear drops onto the table. She takes a deep breath and pulls her hair back from her face.

'It was...Ramage. He was dragging something behind the

52

trailbike, something heavy, attached by a rope. He rode round and round the yard pulling the bundle through the dirt. Then he cut the engine and the dust settled. I heard the woman scream. I wish I had been further away. I wish I didn't know what it was. I wish I'd never seen it. But I did see it. Saw *him*. It was Ken Butler. Most of his clothes had been torn off and his body was raw with blood. But I knew it was him; I could still make out his big white beard. It was...awful.'

I don't know what to say. It's like it's too big to understand. Just yesterday all I had to think about was keeping me and Rowdy fed. But now Rose is here and she's brought trouble.

'They all went inside the store. I so wanted to go down there and do something for Ken. Even just cut the rope, but I knew it was useless. I hoped he was dead. That he wasn't suffering anymore. And I kept thinking over and over, *If he hadn't helped us, he would've still been alive.*'

I'm doing my own thinking. *Maybe I shouldn't have taken her in; maybe she isn't worth the risk.* I'm sure she senses it.

'I'm sorry,' she says. 'I'm sorry I dragged you into this. I'll go.'

She's on her feet, breathing heavily and looking around the kitchen.

'If you could just spare me some food... I'll leave your mum's dress, but there are some old shorts and a jumper in there I could wear.'

She kind of half-smiles, half-grimaces at me. She leans on the table and I can see her arms shaking when she puts her weight on them.

Again, I'm feeling like I have to make a decision too quickly.

The thought of being on my own again suddenly seems unbearable, and the words tumble out without me even thinking about them.

'Stay. Please. We'll work something out. We'll find Kas together. All of us. You, me and Rowdy.'

I've got no idea how we'll do this, or if it's even possible, but I can see the relief in her face. All the weight seems to lift from her shoulders. She sits back down and rests her chin in her hands.

'I'm so tired,' she says.

'There was no sign of a horse when I saw the Wilders this morning,' I say. 'And no sign of a girl. I don't think Kas is with them, but I can go back and check. It's probably a good idea to keep an eye on them, anyway.'

'I'm coming too.'

I know straightaway not to argue with her.

'Wait here.' She disappears into the bedroom. When she comes back she's got different clothes on: a pair of Mum's shorts and a grey woollen jumper that comes halfway down over them. I know it's the right thing to do—to have her wear them—but it still feels strange.

'Too hard to run in a dress,' she says, tugging on the jumper.

'Okay, let's go,' I say. 'Stay close, and if we get separated listen for my whistle.'

I follow the tracks I took this morning, the long way up to the ridge, just in case. Rose follows quietly, but she's not moving as fast as she did yesterday.

Up the top we turn around and look out over the town. I should be checking for danger, but my eyes are drawn to the perfect sets lining up in the river mouth. I haven't even registered that it's offshore. It seems like weeks ago that I was out there surfing those waves. Rose has changed everything.

'I couldn't believe it when I saw you surfing yesterday,' she says.

'It keeps me sane.' I don't say what else I'm thinking: *that it's about the only thing I do that isn't about staying alive.*

'Isn't it dangerous?'

'Nah,' I say. 'There's no danger out there. It's the safest place on earth.'

We turn our backs on the town and follow the ridge up towards the fences. It's about a twenty-minute walk, and we don't speak the whole time. I know Rose's thinking about her sister and what we might find up in the hayshed.

We stay low until we reach the fence. We still can't see anything more than the roof of the shed, so I signal for us to drop back into the bush and climb a tree for a better view. I find the same stringybark from this morning and tap Rowdy gently on the nose. He knows what this means: *stay down, keep quiet.* Then Rose and I climb the tree.

As we get into the higher branches, I lean down to help Rose up. She just looks at me and swings herself onto the branch next to me, even though her injured hand must be hurting.

We peer out through the leaves. The fire is still smoking, but there's only one man sitting by it now. There may be others hidden in the shed. The trailbike is in the same place. Rose puts her finger to her lips and points to our right. Two men are walking along just inside the fence. Rowdy's ears are pricked: he's smelt them, but he hasn't seen them yet. As the men get closer we can hear them talking.

'I'm sick of takin' orders,' one says.

He's a big man, probably a bit over six foot, with a rough beard and hair balding on top. The other one is smaller and he's limping.

Rose taps me on the arm. '*Rat*,' she mouths.

'I'm sick of this wild goose chase. Bein' out here in the cold, night after night. Both the girls are gone. And that scrawny boy's with Warda so they could be anywhere by now.'

'I reckon we should cut our losses and head back to Longley. I'm goin' to have it out with him.'

They veer off towards the hayshed. After a few minutes, we hear shouting and then the sound of something heavy hitting the corrugated iron wall. The big guy we'd just heard talking staggers out into the open and falls on his back. An even bigger man—it must be Ramage—launches at him with a spear in his hand. He lifts it again and again, bringing it down hard into the chest of the man on the ground. The guy's not fighting back anymore. His arms are by his side while his body jerks up and down with every blow. Rose puts her hand on my arm and turns away.

Ramage stands over the body. Then he drops to his knees and takes off the man's boots before walking back into the shed.

I motion to Rose for us to retreat. We climb down and drop

back into the low scrub, Rowdy at our heels. We break into a run when I find the track and before we know it we're back on the ridge, overlooking town.

Finally, we sit down to rest. My heart is pounding. Rose is squeezing her hands between her knees to stop them shaking. Blood is starting to seep through her bandage.

'Do you think he's...?' she whispers.

I want to say no, but we both saw it. 'Dead? Yeah, I think so. Did you recognise him?'

'It was Perkins. He wasn't all bad. He used to sneak food to us at the feedstore. And he never...'

She stares out to the horizon.

'You see what Ramage is like, don't you?' she says, savagely. 'You see why we had to escape?'

'Yeah. But you heard what they said about Kas? They haven't got her. She's safe.'

'No, not safe. She's out there somewhere on her own.'

'But they haven't got her. She's outrun them. We know that much, at least. And she's still on horseback.'

Rose is nodding now. I stand up.

'Let's get home,' I say.

I hold out my hand to help her up. It's another one of those small decisions. She looks at the ground, but this time she does take my hand. She swings to her feet and she's so close I can smell the soap she used to wash her hair this morning.

'Come on, I'm starving,' she says.

Letting go of my hand, she takes off down the track towards the golf course.

5

Back at home we need to do something to take our minds off everything that's happened, at least for a couple of hours. The sun is starting to drop and there's a chill in the air. I start to get dinner ready.

'You ever made rabbit stew?' I ask Rose.

'*Rabbshew*,' she mimics me, smiling, and I notice for the first time the dimple she has on her right cheek. 'Didn't pick you for a cook, Finn.'

'How do you reckon I've stayed alive this long? Eating grass?'

'You're still scrawny.'

'You could do with some fattening up yourself.'

We both go to work on the rabbit stew. I walk through to my veggie patch and pull up an onion and a bulb of garlic. They're only small, but Rose gasps when she sees them.

'You're full of surprises, scrawny boy,' she says.

I should be annoyed, but it seems that suddenly all I want is to hear her talking. Saying anything. Saying my name. I like the way she has to show her teeth to make the *F* sound, the way they sit on her bottom lip.

We stand next to each other and she cuts the onion while I pull the rabbit apart. It's quiet apart from the knife on the bench and the tearing sound of the flesh coming away from the bone. I can feel her there without us even touching.

I start to rub salt into the pieces of rabbit.

'Can I?' she asks.

'What?'

She licks the end of her finger, dips it into the salt and puts it into her mouth. She closes her eyes.

'Salt always reminds me of Stan,' she says. 'He put it on everything. In summer, he'd come in from the paddocks before dinner and open a beer. Just one. He only ever had one stubby. He always had radishes in the fridge. Loved the things. He'd sprinkle salt over them and crunch into them like he was eating apples. "Have one, Rose," he'd say, but they just tasted like salty dirt to me.'

She gazes out through the kitchen window, like Stan might be out there somewhere.

'Stan called you Rose? Not Warda?'

'Rose. Always Rose. What about Finn? Where does that come from?'

I don't want to say, but I'm starting to feel so relaxed with her I can't help myself—anything to keep the conversation going.

'Finbar,' I say. 'It was my grandpa's name. He was Irish.'

'I bet you copped shit at school for that.'

'Yeah. To start with. But everyone got used to it. You know what guys are like with nicknames. Sharkey. That's what they all called me.'

'I like Finn better,' she says.

We fry the onion and garlic in a pan and the kitchen fills with the smell of it, a smell that's linked to memories. Mum and Dad were both good cooks, but Dad's curries were a specialty. The kitchen would be filled with the smell of garlic and onion and then he would put in the curry paste and chillies, and they were so strong that the smell alone could make you cough and sneeze.

When the onion and garlic are nice and brown, I spoon them into a pot with the rabbit pieces, add water, more salt and a precious piece of parsley I picked yesterday. I set the heat to low and we sit back down at the table.

The light is starting to die outside and I realise the day is almost gone. As much as we tried to fill them, the days would sometimes drag when it was just Rowdy and me. Now, with Rose here, time seems to be moving so much faster.

The stew starts to bubble in the pot. I know the cooking has just been a distraction. We'll have to figure out how we can find Kas and bring her here.

'Tell me what happened after Swan's Marsh. If we're going to sort out a plan for finding Kas, I need more to go on.'

As soon as I say this, all her calm seems to dissolve and she looks agitated, her knees jigging under the table again.

'By the time I got clear of the town buildings, Kas and the horse were gone,' she says. 'I knew Ramage and his men would figure out what had happened soon enough and they'd follow me. I didn't care—if they were looking for me that meant they weren't looking for Kas. But there was no sign of her. The next morning it pissed with rain. I kept listening for the sound of the trailbike. The road wound up through the forest to the top of the ridge. There's an old camp ground up there.'

I know this spot well. It's called Pinchgut Junction. Two forest tracks go off in either direction along the line of the ridge, while the main road goes straight up and over the top before it drops towards the coast.

'The road passes through a big cutting,' Rose continues. 'It was the perfect spot to ambush anyone on the road. I wasn't going to walk through it so I climbed to the top of the cutting. When I looked over the edge, sure enough, men were there. Then everything went quiet—and I couldn't believe what I saw. Kas was riding her horse right into the cutting. And she had someone on the back with her. I don't know who it was—boy or girl—but they looked about the same size as Kas. I didn't even think. I stood up and yelled at Kas that it was a trap. Just as I did, Ramage's men came out into the open. I threw some rocks at them, then I ran along the top so they'd follow me. I wanted to draw them away from Kas. My plan worked, kind of. They did come—but now I had to outrun them.'

The kitchen window is fogged up with the steam from the pot. I pull the blinds down, light the candle and set it on the table between us. Rose leans forward in her chair and rubs her eyes.

'Kas could be anywhere by now, Finn. And it's all my fault. I acted like an idiot at Swan's Marsh, took a stupid, dumb risk. We should've stuck together.'

'Well, you can't do anything about that now,' I say. 'At least we know she's not alone; there was someone else on the horse.'

'But just some other kid.'

'Okay, but she's got a better chance than if she was on her own.'

'Maybe.'

'And she knows the plan was to head south if you got split up, so she could still be trying to get through. She knows not to try to go through Pinchgut Junction again.'

Rose must know this is making sense, but it doesn't stop her fretting. She's picking at the bandage on her hand again.

'We can't do anything tonight, anyway,' I say. 'We both need to sleep. If we're going to try to find her, we'll need all the energy we can get.'

Rose doesn't argue, and the smell of the stew has filled the kitchen. She's tired; her eyes are starting to droop and she cups her hands under her chin.

I turn to the sink, pour us glasses of water and put them on the table. They're a bit murky, which means the header tank must be getting low. I remind myself to pump some more water up to it tomorrow.

'How old are you?' she asks, suddenly, like it's the most important question ever.

'Almost sixteen by now,' I say, easing myself into the chair. 'What about you?'

'Nineteen, I suppose.'

'I'd just started at a new school, Wentworth High, when it all started.'

Rose gasps. 'You were a Wentworth wanker?'

I laugh. 'Yeah, a Wentworth wanker. But where'd you hear that? You said you weren't allowed to go to school.'

'From one of the girls at the feedstore. Her name was Caroline. She went to some exclusive girls' school before...'

'Probably Scarborough,' I say. 'Scarborough skanks, we called them.'

It makes me stop for a bit—thinking about school, how organised and regular it all was. Bells and timetables, start and finish times. The way every day was so neatly divided up.

'My whole life was sport and surfing and school. Mucking around. Me and my mates would surf every day, stay out till it was too dark to see the sets, then paddle in and head home for dinner. The weekends were footy and hanging around the netball courts to watch the girls. Pretty normal stuff.'

'Perving!' she says.

'Kinda,' I say, a bit embarrassed. 'I took it all for granted, but who doesn't when that's all you know? Who expects a disease to rip through and kill everyone? Then the survivors all clear out and leave you behind.'

Rowdy gets to his feet and nuzzles up against my leg. I scratch him in his favourite spot under his chin, and he lets out a dog moan. Then he sniffs at Rose's feet and nudges her with his nose.

'Where's the spot you scratch him?' she asks.

I move around the table to show her. Next thing Rowdy has his nose in her lap and looks as contented as can be.

'We had four working dogs on the farm,' Rose says. 'Leela, Hamish, Coco and Archie. All kelpies. They were never allowed in the house. But I used to make cosy spots for them in the hayshed so they could keep warm in winter.'

'I don't know where I would've been without Rowdy. He's the best mate I've ever had.'

Rose looks around the kitchen—as though she's seeing it for the first time—before her eyes come to rest on me again.

'Still, it must have been tough,' she says, finally. 'So long on your own.'

I've never wanted to admit being lonely; it only made things worse if I stewed on it. But now, with Rose here, it's like I can let it go.

'Yeah,' I say. 'It was.'

We clear the table to eat. I think about where to sit—next to her or at the other end of the table? Sharing our stories has made me more comfortable with her being here. It feels like she's opening up, but I'm still trying to piece together everything she's told me.

I dish up the stew. Rose eats slower this time, using the knife and fork instead of her hands. She seems distracted though, fiddling with her food.

'I've got to find Kas,' she says at last. 'I can't think about anything else. I don't expect you to help. I've brought you enough trouble already. Ramage knows you're here and he knows I'm with you. He'll be back with more men and they'll track us down. They'll bring dogs.'

I wipe my mouth with the back of my hand. 'I don't get it about Ramage,' I say. 'Why is he so determined to find you?'

Rose won't look at me.

'Sorry,' she mutters. 'There's stuff I just can't tell you. Not yet.'

I must have been wrong about the trust building between us. I know she can see I'm hurt, but I want her to feel it. I've risked everything for her, taken her in, fed her and now she's holding out on me.

'I thought we—'

'Ah, Finn,' she says in a tired voice that makes her sound so much older than me. 'I'm so grateful. You saved me yesterday. And you've treated me so nicely, I feel like I owe you.'

'So tell me, then.'

'There's stuff I can't bring myself to talk about. And none of it will help me find Kas.'

She stirs her stew.

'I'm going to leave tomorrow to look for her. Please don't feel you need to come. I'll be okay.'

I'm shaking my head. I've already made my decision about going with her. 'We need to think this through,' I say. 'Kas could still be heading down here, towards the coast. We could miss her and end up getting caught ourselves.'

Rose doesn't have an answer to this and I feel as though I've had a small victory.

'You'd better eat your stew before it goes cold,' I say.

She looks down at the bowl as though she's forgotten it's there, then starts eating again. This gives me a chance to think, to convince her to stay for a few days longer to see if Kas arrives. When she lifts the fork to her mouth I see how dirty and stained the bandage is where she stitched her hand. She keeps flexing her fingers and the lower half of her arm is red and swollen.

'We need to change that bandage, too.'

'It feels strange,' she says, finishing her last mouthful of stew and unwinding the bandage. 'My fingers keep twitching and it's like my whole arm's got pins and needles.'

The last part of the bandage has stuck to the skin and she winces as it peels away. The wound itself is almost black and where she's pushed the needle through the skin is bright red. I feel my heart quicken. The infection is spreading up her arm.

'That doesn't look good,' I murmur.

I remember there are some antibiotics in the bathroom that I brought over from the old house. I kick myself for not having thought of them earlier.

In the cabinet I find a dozen different capsule containers and I try to think of the name of the ones I took when I had tonsillitis years ago. I know we had some left over. For some reason the name *Eric* is in my head. Mum used to say, 'Finn, it's time for *Eric*.' The labels are faded and some are unreadable. I take them all out and line them up on the kitchen table.

'Maybe we should just take a lucky dip,' Rose says. She starts to read the labels. 'Celebrex, Toradol, Erythro...Erythromycin.'

'That's it! Eric!' I say. 'It's an antibiotic.'

'There's two bottles of it—not much in this one,' she says, shaking it, 'but this one's full.' She studies the label. 'They're way past the use-by date, but they've got to be better than nothing.'

Afterwards she allows me to dress her hand. I tear up an old sheet for a bandage and clean the stitches in warm water before squeezing more antiseptic cream onto the wound. I can see the hairs standing up on her forearm.

'Take two of the antibiotics now,' I say, 'and another couple first thing in the morning, I reckon. We'll have to be real careful with the infection. I don't think we should travel until it's under control. Maybe a week?'

'No way,' she says, the edge finding its way back into her voice. 'I'm leaving tomorrow.'

She's glaring at me with sharp eyes again, but the pain must be playing on her mind. It's something I've worried about for as long as I've been on my own: getting really sick and not having anyone here to look after me. Or getting bitten by a snake out in the bush or stung by a blue-ringed octopus when I'm feeling around for crabs in the rock pools.

The candle gives a last splutter and we are thrown into the dark. I can't see Rose across the table, but I hear her yawn.

'You should get some sleep,' I say. 'I'll go and do a check around the neighbourhood.'

She says goodnight and I see her silhouette shuffle down the hall to the bedroom. I slip out the back door and head for the beach, keeping to the back tracks, just in case.

I make it to the platform above the river mouth as the moon begins to rise over the cliffs out towards Red Rock Point. The wind is still offshore and I can just make out the whitewater peeling along the sandbar. I can tell by the sound it makes when it crashes on the inside bar that it's still pretty solid, maybe four or five feet. If there's no sign of the Wilders in the morning, I'll paddle out early and grab a few waves to clear my head.

6

It's barely light when I wake up. Rose had been tossing and turning all night, at one stage calling out a name I didn't recognise.

I tiptoe up the hallway to check on her.

She doesn't look good. Even from the doorway I can see she's feverish: her hair is wet and she's half in and half out of the blanket. But she's asleep and that's a good thing. Her head is turned away from the door and the singlet she's wearing has slipped off her shoulder. I wonder if it's such a good idea to leave her alone, but I figure I won't be long and she'll probably sleep through anyway.

I walk quietly out of the house. I figure the board I left on the beach when Rose arrived would have been washed away, so I grab one of Dad's old ones from the shed. My wetsuit is still damp.

Rowdy slips through the shed door ahead of me and dances around my legs. Up on the platform overlooking the beach I change into my wetsuit and stash my clothes in the tea tree. I climb to the top of the highest dune and scan upriver as the first light creeps into the day. There's no sign of movement and Rowdy hasn't picked up any new scents on the breeze.

Out on the beach, it's like stepping back to my old life—just me, my board, Rowdy and a peeling right-hander at the river mouth.

The first duck dive under the shore break slaps me in the face and wakes me up. I pop out the other side and start to dig in with long strokes. Once I make it to clear water I take a few deep breaths and slow my paddling to an easy flow. I stay to the right of the peak and allow the current to carry me into position in the take-off zone. The swell has built since last night and the sets are lining up on the sandbar.

As I wait, I scan the beach and look as far up the river towards town as I can. There is a low mist sitting on the water. A big old pelican glides in like a jumbo jet, sticking his feet out at the last minute to slice through the surface of the water and ease to a halt. The sun is just starting to catch the trees up on the tips of the ridge, turning them a burnt orange. Rowdy is prowling the sand looking for the next seagull to chase. When

I look back out to sea, the horizon has disappeared behind the approaching set.

I roll over the top of the first wave because I know the ones deeper in the set will be bigger and more powerful. The third one is peaking perfectly so I paddle straight at it, pivot my board at the last second, dig a couple of big strokes in and feel the strength of it lift and carry me forwards.

Now everything is in its place and the earth is back on its axis. There's no virus, no one trying to kill me, no orphan kid battling to stay alive. There's just this wave and me. It's travelled across thousands of kilometres of ocean just to get here and its journey has almost come to an end.

I drop down the wave and lean in towards the face, arching my body to drive off the bottom. The board responds and I feel the power again, like I've been hurled out of a slingshot. Out on the shoulder I dig my rail and plant my back foot to cut back towards the whitewater. Dad always said that every surfer has a move that defines them. This is it, my signature. The cut-back sends out an arc of spray that catches the morning light.

I bounce off the whitewater and bring the board back around to the face before surging off again, repeating the moves over and over until the wave is exhausted and crashes on the sand.

I lose all sense of time when I'm in the water. I may have surfed for one hour or three, but the sun is well above the ridge now, so I need to paddle in and get back to the business of staying alive.

I'm so relaxed I forget to birdcall to let Rose know I'm back. When I step out of the shed she's standing a few metres away with an arrow pulled tight in the bow, pointed at my chest.

'Shit, Finn! Where have you been?'

She eases the tension on the bow and points the arrow to the ground. She's sweating and shaking.

'Sorry. I've been for a surf.'

'A surf? There are Wilders hunting us, I'm feeling like shit and you go for a surf! What are you thinking, you stupid little boy?'

She's screaming.

'Sorry,' I say again, 'I didn't mean to...'

'I didn't know where you were. You've got to tell me if you're going to disappear like that. For all I know you could've... I was scared.'

With that, she collapses to her knees. Her hair is wet with perspiration. I crouch in front of her and touch her shoulder. Her skin is on fire.

'Come on,' I say. 'Let's go inside.'

She lets me carry her into the house. We go straight to the bathroom and I tell her to get into the bath. She's too exhausted to argue.

When I lift the heavy jumper over her shoulders she leans forward and hugs her knees to her chest. She's wearing only shorts and a singlet underneath.

I turn on the tap and the bath begins to fill with precious water from the tank I know is already low. Rose shivers when the water touches her skin but she doesn't try to climb out.

Slowly it creeps over her legs and inches up towards her waist.

'That's enough,' she croaks. 'We can't afford too much.'

With a cup from the kitchen I begin to pour water over her head and shoulders. She leans back slightly and allows me to put a wet cloth on her forehead. I unwrap the bandage, which is almost black with caked blood, and give the wound a good clean.

'It looks better,' I say, trying to sound convincing. 'You'll have a nice scar to show for it.'

'At least it's one I can see,' she says.

When the shivering takes over her whole body, I help Rose up and wrap a towel around her shoulders. Embarrassed, she turns her back to me.

'Rose,' I say, 'we have to take these wet clothes off and get you into bed.'

She nods. She turns to face me as I pull her singlet up over her head. The ring falls between her breasts and she puts an arm over her chest. Her body is a mess of bruises and cuts, but that's not what grabs my attention. I can hardly believe what I'm seeing.

She's pregnant.

She sees me looking and turns her head away. I take down the pair of Mum's shorts she's still wearing from yesterday. Her hand comes down to cover herself again.

'Don't look,' she says.

I hesitate. 'You gotta trust me. I'm not going to hurt you,' I say, quietly.

Eventually, her arms drape over my shoulders, and we half

walk, half stumble to the bedroom. She drops onto the bed and I pull the blanket over her. Her eyes are trying to focus and she grabs hold of my arm.

'I was going to tell you, Finn. I was.'

'It's okay. We'll talk about it later.'

I'm still too shocked to know what else to say. All I can think is *fuck!*

At last she closes her eyes and I sit with her until her hand slips off my arm and she sleeps.

I'm restless all day. I keep chopping and changing my mind, going in to check on Rose, sitting with her but the whole time just wanting to run away, to hide somewhere, to talk to someone who'll know what to do. Everything feels like it's falling in on me—Rose has come, the Wilders have seen me, and now she's sick. And pregnant. I'm in so much danger but I can't stand the thought of being on my own again.

I keep an eye on Rose, bringing damp cloths to put on her forehead. Sometimes she responds by making little noises or breathing in deep, but mostly she doesn't move at all. In the afternoon I wake her up and force her to drink. I've broken open the antibiotic capsules and dissolved them in water. She manages to keep it down, but the fever seems to be getting worse.

By nightfall, I'm exhausted and starving. I haven't eaten all day. I get a can of soup out of the shed, boil up some of the rabbit bones from yesterday to make a stock, and combine them all together. I add some salt to make it a bit more edible. When it's all cooked I take a bowl into Rose and prop her up on the pillows. She tries to push me away but she's got no strength left in her body. She pulls the blanket up to her shoulders and holds it there while I spoon some soup into her mouth. It's like trying to feed a baby—she keeps turning her head away.

'Come on. You've got to eat.'

'Not hungry,' she murmurs.

'Please.' I must sound angry.

'Ah, Finn,' she says. 'You don't know anything about me. You don't know what I've done. You wouldn't like me if I told you.'

It seems to take all her effort just to get this out.

I try to keep her focused. 'We have to find Kas. She's relying on us. But first you've got to get better.'

Rose lifts her arm, puts it around my shoulder and draws me into her. My face is against her skin and I feel how hot and clammy it is.

'Help me, Finn,' she whispers. 'Just help me.'

She drifts off again, and I ease her back into the bed.

Out in the kitchen I sit and stare at the tabletop. Rowdy comes over and lays his head in my lap. I miss Mum and Dad all of a sudden, their adult way of making things right.

I remember Dad's story of the day I was born. Mum went into labour really quickly and they had to make a dash for the hospital in their old Kombi van. They only made it halfway when Mum yelled to Dad that he had to pull over, the baby was coming. He climbed into the back and sure enough, I was entering the world right there on the back seat. Dad picked me up, made sure I was breathing and handed me to Mum. Then he got back behind the wheel and drove us to the hospital.

He first told me this story when I was only about six or seven, and he made it sound like a big adventure with a happy-ever-after ending. When I was a bit older, though, he told me more about that day. He said he didn't get emotional until we were safely in the hospital. Then it all hit him in a rush and he felt completely buggered. But when things were at their most critical he said he knew he had to keep a cool head. There was a job to do and he was responsible, though Mum always rolled her eyes at him thinking he was the one doing all the hard work.

I know there's a job to be done here and I don't have the time to get emotional about it. I need to clear my head. In the meantime I have to make sure Rose doesn't get any worse. And the weirdest thing is I feel like I have to make it up to her for all the bad things other people have done to her.

Dad's voice keeps ringing in my ears about the first thing you do when you have to make a decision—you put together a list. So I sit down at the kitchen table and get out a pencil and paper. There've been things stacking up that I've forgotten about. So I start with them.

1. The traps.

They're still up along the fence line where I left them yesterday. This'll be risky. The Wilders might have found them by now and realised I'll be back to check them. I wish I hadn't reset them when I caught my last lot of rabbits.

2. Food.

I can't keep drawing on the supplies in the shed at this rate.

I need fresh food. I haven't been looking after myself the last few days. I'll be useless to Rose if I get sick too.

3. Ray.

I haven't been out to see him in a couple of weeks. He'll be worried. If I check the traps first, I might get lucky and have a rabbit to take for him. I can trade for some veggies and I need to tell him about Rose, too. He'll have a better idea of how to look after her.

4. Kas.

I don't even know her yet but she's going to need help. Once Rose is well enough to travel she'll want to look for her sister anyway, so best to get organised for the trip and work out what I need to carry.

Somehow I have to do all of this and look after Rose at the same time. I'm not even sure she'd understand me if I tried to explain it to her. I consider slipping off and getting something done while she's asleep, but I don't want her to wake up alone again.

And then, of course, there's the thing I don't want to even think about. She's pregnant. At least it makes more sense of her story—the vomiting, what she told me about Longley, their escape and Ramage's mission to recapture her. I can't help wondering how she got pregnant. Was it a Wilder?

When I look in on Rose, she's asleep. She's pushed the blanket back and the sheet clings to her body. I get the cloth again and bring a bucket of water to her bed. She stirs when I start wiping her face, her eyes opening for a few seconds.

'So hot,' she murmurs.

I don't know what to say so I keep dipping the cloth in the water and sponging her down. Her hand strokes her belly.

'I didn't know how to tell you,' she says.

Tears well in her eyes but there's anger behind them too.

'What am I going to do?' she asks.

'I've worked out a plan,' I say. 'I'll be in and out to see that you're okay, but I've gotta get things organised. I'm going to head out this arvo and see Ray. Remember I told you about him? He'll be able to help us.'

She's drifting off again.

'Finn,' she manages to say, 'you talk so much.'

A faint smile crosses her lips before she falls asleep.

7

Rowdy and I scout the long way again, out past the golf course that's gradually being reclaimed by the bush. It takes about half an hour to get up to the fence and this time I approach cautiously, staying low and crawling to take advantage of the bracken fern for cover.

Up closer, I signal to Rowdy and he drops to his haunches and waits. Everything's quiet. To my right I can see a rabbit in one of the traps. It's still alive, pawing at the ground with its front legs to try to escape the metal jaws. It's the only sign of movement up here. Even the wind has backed off; the trees are still.

I scuttle back into the scrub and make my way parallel to the fence until I find the tree from yesterday. Rowdy drops at the base of the trunk while I climb into the canopy. There's still no sign of life, no smoke from a fire and no body of the man attacked by Ramage yesterday.

I climb down and walk back towards the rabbit in the trap. I'm about ten metres from it when Rowdy freezes. His ears are pricked and the hair on the back of his neck is bristling.

'What is it boy?' I whisper, dropping to my stomach. Rowdy holds his position. I pop my head up just above the ferns and scan the paddock. Nothing. But as I drop down again, I see it. Just in front of the rabbit in the trap is a mound of leaves in a circle. I probably wouldn't have seen it if I was standing up, but at ground level I can see it's an unnatural shape and there are boot marks around it. There's a piece of rope snaking off to a tree branch that's been bent down and tied to a metal peg in the ground. It's a trap—and it's meant for me.

I don't know if they are watching, but I figure if they were they'd probably have made a move by now. I edge around the booby trap, scramble in to get the rabbit, free it from the jaws and quickly stretch its neck. I can't risk losing the trap so I pull it up, shake the dirt off it and place it carefully in my backpack, followed by the rabbit. The other four traps are all further along the fence so I follow it until I find them too. They're all empty, and I trigger each with a piece of wood and stash them in a hollow log, hoping I'm not disturbing a snake.

I can move freely again without the weight of the traps and

I make good time down into a gully before I pick up the trail that will lead me to the cliff tops and out along the coast to Ray's valley.

This is the quickest way to Ray's, but it's also the most dangerous. The track is exposed because the bush ends and the low heathland takes over a couple of hundred metres back from the edge. Anyone hanging back in the tree line will be able to see me, but I just have to take the risk.

The sun is starting to drop—I know I have to hurry. Ray may not answer my signal if I get there past dark. I'm not worried about making my way home at night; I reckon I could do the trip blindfolded.

It starts to rain, but it's thin and misty—not enough to hide me. Rowdy senses the danger and moves along close to my leg. There's a stretch of about five hundred metres that gives no cover, so we break into a steady run. The rain thickens and low cloud rolls in.

I'm getting used to operating like this, with adrenaline pumping through me. I used to get my thrills riding my bike down the steep tracks off the ridge or surfing big waves out on the point, but now it's just how I live, on edge, pushing against the fear the whole time.

It's tough going through the heathland, but we make headway, and after about half an hour Red Rocks Point appears out of the mist. Rowdy bounds ahead to the top and waits for me to climb up. The granite slopes back into the bush and pretty soon we're fighting our way through waist-high bracken. Eventually we find an animal track that leads inland. The rain has eased and the sky brightens as the low sun finds a path through the clouds.

When I've come out to see Ray before, I've always approached from the other direction, coming down into the valley from the coast road. I'm a bit unsure of my directions today, but I figure if I keep moving uphill I can't go too far wrong. I have to find his place before dark.

When the trees start to thin a little, I make out the glint of corrugated iron on the other side of a creek that splits the valley. Rowdy and I cross over and keep low as we approach the clearing below a shed. I want to be sure it's safe before we go any further.

Coming from the north, there's a trip-wire set up, attached to an old cowbell on his front porch. But we're arriving from the coast and I'm not sure Ray's got any warning mechanism from this direction. The only reason he's survived so long here on his own is that his farm is cut off from any roads. It was the back block of a bigger farm up on the coast road. The scrub has reclaimed most of the other farm's paddocks, forming a perfect screen for Ray's place.

I ease through the fence and make a quick dash for the cover of the shed, Rowdy running by my side. From here I can see up across the furrows of the back paddock and the raised veggie beds closer to the house. It all looks quiet. There's nothing but open ground between us and the back porch—about fifty metres, I reckon. We have to make a run for it. Once I get closer to the house I'll call out to Ray so we don't surprise him.

I grab Rowdy by the collar so he won't get ahead of me

and we're just about to break cover when I hear the click of a shotgun being cocked.

'You wanna be more careful, Finn. Someone'll blow ya brains out one day.'

'Jesus, you scared the shit out of me.'

Ray lowers the shottie. 'Why're you coming from the south, young fella? Not your usual way.'

'Sorry, I had to come along the coast. Quickest way.'

He looks at me warily, sensing trouble.

'You being tracked?' His eyes shift back to the bush beyond the fence.

I'm short of breath, gulping for air. He grabs me by the collar and pulls me back into the shed.

'What's going on?'

'It's Wilders. Half-a-dozen of them. Been hanging around for a couple of days since—'

'Since what?'

Ray's the only other person I've spoken to in years, the only other person I can trust.

'Can we go up to the house?' I ask. 'I wasn't followed, I'm sure of it.'

He looks at me in the fading light and smiles.

'Come on then,' he says, 'you look like a drowned rat.'

We cross the paddock quickly, or as quick as Ray can go. I reckon he must be in his seventies by now and each winter he seems to get a little slower. He walks a bit like a crab, with his bowed legs keeping his body close to the ground.

Ray's house leans to one side where the stumps have given

way. There are exposed floorboards, an old combustion stove and chipped cups on hooks on a dresser that looks like it could fall apart at any minute. He stands the shotgun in the corner and eases himself into a battered armchair in front of the stove. Rowdy sidles up to him and Ray scratches him behind the ears. He's always had a soft spot for Rowdy.

'Now, you'd better tell me what's going on,' he says.

'There's a girl. She was chased into town the day before yesterday by a pack of Wilders. She's safe, she's at my place, but she's crook. She's got a bad cut on her hand and it's infected.'

'A girl! She got the virus?'

'Don't think so. I'm pretty sure it's the cut that's the problem. She's got a bad fever.'

'Where'd she come from?'

I take a deep breath and tell him as much of Rose's story as I can remember, including that Kas is still out there. He listens carefully. After two winters it's almost beyond belief that this could happen. I reckon he's sizing up how all this might affect him, whether he's safe or in more danger because of what I've done. When I'm finished, he sits for a long time, thinking.

'Bloody hell,' he finally says. 'That's a game changer.'

There's something reassuring in the way he says this. It's getting darker, but I think I can see a smile on his face.

'There's something else, Ray. She's pregnant.'

'Jesus, Mary and Joseph! Are you sure?'

'She's sure.'

'How old is she?'

'Nineteen.'

Ray sits quietly, scratching his beard. The rain has started up again, bouncing off the corrugated iron roof.

'I'm not sure what help I can be,' he says. 'I don't know much about babies. You know me and Harriet never had any kids. Not for want of trying, mind you.' There's a chuckle in his voice.

'I've got no idea about babies either,' I say. 'I know where they come from, but not anything about helping someone *have* a baby.'

'How many months do you reckon she is?'

'Dunno. She didn't say. You can see her belly's swollen, though.'

'All right. You know Harriet was a nurse? She would've known what to do. Pretty sure there're still some of her textbooks somewhere we can dig out. But it sounds as though we've gotta get the girl through this fever first.'

I like the way Ray is saying *we*. I remember the rabbit in my bag and get it out for him.

'It's not much, but I've been a bit pressed for time. He's a freshy, though. Caught this morning.'

'Good lad. I've been missing my bunny stews. I've got a jar of honey for you. Cleaned out the hive yesterday. And how're you off for spuds and carrots?'

'Run out. Just a few onions and some garlic and parsley in the garden.'

'All right, then. Bring me some of that parsley when you come out next,' he says, rummaging around in a sack on the floor. 'Here's a few spuds and I pulled the carrots yesterday.

The girl'll need lots of fluid. Soups, that sort of thing. And...'

He stops mid-sentence.

'Wait here.' He gets to his feet slowly, heads out the back door and is gone for a good ten minutes. When he reappears, he's holding a chicken by its legs, its body limp, its neck wobbling against his thigh. I can't remember when I last ate chicken. I haven't wanted to kill the wild ones around town because I like the eggs. I know Ray's only got a few left that haven't been taken by foxes.

'You didn't have to do that, Ray.'

'It's all right. Let's get that girl well again. Whenever I was crook Harriet made up the best chicken soup. Boil it up with the veggies and force her to eat it, if you have to. Keep the bones for stock. Mix the honey with hot water and give it to her. And when she's well enough, bring her out to meet me. Then we'll work out how to find her sister.'

I can't help it. I throw my arms around him in the dark and hug him. He rocks on his feet then leans in and holds me tight. We've never done this before, but it seems like things are changing, like Rose's arrival might mean there's more hope. Even if the hope is mixed with danger.

He ruffles my hair. 'From what you've told me, she's a tough little bugger. She'll pull through. Now,' he says, 'you'd best get going before it gets too dark.'

'Thanks so much, Ray.'

'You look after yourself, young fella,' Ray says when Rowdy and I are ready to leave. Then he smiles and says, 'I see you're talking a bit better. I'm guessing she's been at you about it?'

'What'd you mean?'

'Well, y'know, you always talked a bit strange, kinda half-boy, half-dog.'

'You never said anything about it before.'

'Didn't see the point. I could understand you just the same.'

I've got the chicken in my backpack and Rowdy's dancing around, going apeshit with the smell of it. It's dark now, but a quarter-moon has risen. We're halfway across the front paddock when Ray calls.

'What's her name?'

'Rose,' I call back.

'Like the flower.'

'Yeah,' I say. 'Like the flower.'

8

I don't want to scare Rose when I get back so I wait out by the shed and whistle a couple of times. When there's no response, I figure she's asleep and go through the back door into the kitchen.

It's somehow darker inside. I grab the torch off the kitchen bench and, leaving it switched off, make my way to Rose's room. I almost trip on something big and soft on the floor. My heart jumps when I flick the torch on to find Rose lying across the doorway.

She flinches with the light. There's spew on the floor and her whole body, wrapped and twisted in a sheet, is wet.

Rowdy slips past me and starts nuzzling into her, licking her face. She groans and tries to push herself up against the doorframe.

I help her to sit up. She breathes out heavily and wipes her hand across her face.

'Rose, are you okay?'

'No sign of Kas?'

'No, not yet. Let's get you back into bed. I've got some food from Ray.'

'I've made a mess. Spewed everywhere.'

'That's okay. We'll put you in my bed. Then I can clean up in here.'

She's too weak to argue, but she does ask me to turn off the torch. In the dark she allows me to lift her up and unwind her body from the sheet. She's naked. I try to prop her against the wall, but her whole weight falls into me and I can feel her breasts and belly pushing against me. Her arms are around my neck, and I lift her off her feet and carry her down the hallway. She is so light; I can't work out whether she's lost weight since she got here or if she was like that when she arrived. All I'm conscious of is her face pushed into my chest and her small gasps for air.

I lower her onto my bed as carefully as I can and pull the covers over her.

'We'll be okay, Finn, won't we?' she whispers.

'Yeah, course. But let me look at your hand again, and change the bandage. And you need to have some more of the antibiotics.'

Heading back to the kitchen I look into the other room. The stench is pretty gross and the bed is wet through.

When I come back, Rose is drowsy, but she drinks the water with the tablets while I unwrap her wound. It's still inflamed and there's pus congealed along the line of the stitches.

'You'd make a great nurse,' she murmurs, and attempts a smile as I begin to clean it.

'I don't think it's any worse. The antibiotics might be starting to kick in.'

'Hmm. Hope so.'

This is the last thing she says before she heaves a sigh and falls asleep. She's got the sheet pulled up to her chin and her hair, all knotted and tangled, spreads across the pillow. I want to touch her face, but she looks so peaceful and calm that I leave her and go start the tidy up.

It takes a while to strip the bed, clean the floor and mop up. I'm stuffed after everything that's happened today—until I remember the chicken. I need to deal with it while it's fresh.

It's a long and dirty job, and it's getting on by the time I finish. Finally, I give in to the exhaustion. The empty room still smells like spew, so I drag the mattress in next to Rose and lay it on the floor. I convince myself I need to be here if she wakes up, but really I just want to lie and listen to her breathing.

I'm woken in the morning by something sharp sticking into my ribs. I roll over, but there's something on the other side too. I open my eyes. Rose is looking down from her bed.

'When did you start growing feathers?' she says, grinning.

'What?'

I sit up and I'm covered in little feathers from plucking the chicken in the dark last night. I brush them off as best I can.

'How you feeling?' I ask.

'Bit better, I think,' she says. 'Tired.'

There's colour in her face and her eyes look brighter.

'What happened yesterday?' she asks. 'And where'd all those feathers come from?'

Now I grin. 'Ray. He gave us a chicken. He wants to meet you. Wants to help us, if he can. He can't travel, but as soon as you get well enough we'll go out and visit him.'

'Chicken? A real chicken?'

'No, a rubber one. With feathers.'

This makes her laugh. 'You're an idiot!'

And more than anything else, more than the antibiotics and the chicken and Ray's offer to help, this laugh makes me think she's going to be okay. We are going to be okay. She's weak and I can see her arm is still swollen, but it's like something has turned. She lies back on the pillow and I think she's gone to sleep again, but when I get up her eyes are open. She's staring at the ceiling.

'I dreamed of Kas last night,' she says. 'She was here, safe with us.'

'We'll find her. I promise.'

'I'm so weak I'd only slow you down. I was thinking... Maybe you could go and look for her on your own? You'll have a better chance of finding her. In a day or so I'll be able to look after myself here. There's enough food.'

I sit on the edge of the bed. 'But what if the Wilders come? You won't be able to run. Or defend yourself.'

'We have to take that chance. Kas's been on her own out there for three days now.'

'Not on her own, remember? She's got someone with her.'

Rose snorts. 'Yeah, another *kid*. They'll be no help against Ramage.'

It's hard to argue with her logic. She would slow me down and there's every chance the infection could come back if she doesn't rest. I know the country this side of Pinchgut Junction well enough to stay off the roads. It worries me that I've only got a vague idea of where Kas might be, but it's a chance I might just have to take. I could take some food from here and hunt along the way.

'There's something else, Finn.' There's a quiver in her voice now. 'I'm more pregnant than I look; about six months, I reckon. Maybe more.'

'Does Kas know?'

'Yeah,' Rose says, quietly. 'I had to tell someone. She'll be worried sick.'

I walk out into the kitchen. This plan seems to make sense, though I need to work it through in my mind. Rose will have to look after herself while I'm gone. But what's the alternative? It could take another couple of weeks for her to be well enough to travel and that's another couple of weeks further into her pregnancy. She's only going to get slower and there's always the possibility of harming the baby. Or worse: both of us being caught by Ramage and his men. Maybe I can draw Rose a map to Ray's place and if I'm not back in a week she could go out there on her own?

All of this is streaming through my head as I cut the chicken into pieces and put it into a big pot with the last of the onion and garlic, along with a couple of Ray's carrots and potatoes. I'd prefer to roast it all. I can't remember when I last had roast chicken, but I know the soup will be easier for Rose to eat. And if I go ahead with the plan I can take some of the meat with me.

Once I've turned the gas on and set it to cooking, I look in on Rose. She's sleeping. The light is coming in through a crack in the curtains and it's spilling across the bed. She's got one shoulder out of the sheets now and the sun catches the little hairs at the back of her neck.

The smell of the soup soon fills the house. I sit back at the table and put my head on my arms. I must doze for a few minutes because the next thing I know Rose, wrapped in a sheet, is shaking me.

She puts her fingers to her lips. 'Shh. Listen.'

At first all I can hear is the wind in the trees, but then, when it dies down for a few seconds, I hear the unmistakable sound of a motor. A trailbike. Not revving out, just putting along, like they're taking their time, checking things out.

The first thing I do is turn the gas off and put the pot with the chicken into the bottom cupboard. If we can smell it in here, they might be able to out there as well. Then I draw all the blinds.

Rose has the same look on her face as she had when I first saw her on the beach: fear and anger rolled into one. She pulls me down onto the floor, then huddles against me. Rowdy gets up and growls, his tail and ears standing to attention. I motion him over to us and we hold onto him like a life jacket in the ocean.

We can hear voices but they're not close yet, maybe twenty metres away, which would put them out by the front gate. I know they won't be able to see our place. There's a screen of tea tree across what used to be the access track from the road to our house at the back of the block.

After a few minutes they move off down the street towards the river, the *put-put* of the trailbike dropping out of earshot. I decide to go and check things out.

I scout through the yards of the houses lower down the street and find a spot where I can get a view closer to the river. The trailbike has gone ahead of the pack—about five Wilders I can count from here—to what looks like a makeshift camp on the riverbank. Smoke rises from a fire and furniture that must've been pulled out of nearby houses is arranged around it. The men wander across the main road and they all huddle around the fire.

Back in the house Rose is still sitting on the kitchen floor.

'What's happening?'

'They're camping down on the riverbank.'

94

Her shoulders slump forward as another glimmer of hope is snuffed out. I try to stay positive, though I know this is a disaster. We can't stay here and I can't leave Rose. The Wilders will eventually find us and our stores.

'It's my fault,' she says. 'I've brought you too much trouble already. Maybe I should just hand myself in and go back to Longley with them.'

'Give up, you mean?'

I don't intend it to sound so aggressive. She sticks her chin out and some of the defiance returns to her eyes.

'If things are going to fuck up,' I say, 'let's at least make it hard for them.'

She smiles at this.

'So, the first thing,' I say, 'is to finish cooking the chicken. But I have to check the wind first.'

The north-westerly has picked up, meaning the smell of the cooking will be pushed away from the riverbank where the Wilders are camped. I get the pot out of the cupboard, put it back on the stove and light the jets. My mind is racing, trying to see a way that will keep Rose safe, get the Wilders to leave and give me the chance to find Kas.

But it's Rose, sitting up at the table again, who speaks first.

'The trailbike,' she says. 'That's the problem. Without that, you could outrun them, lead them away from town. You need to get them to follow you, but they have to be on foot. Like you.'

'Not on *foot*...'

I can't believe I haven't thought of it before.

'I've got my mountain bike back at our old house. In the

shed. I haven't used it because I never needed to go far and it was useless for hunting. If we can damage the trailbike in some way, I can easily outrun them. They must have petrol somewhere to keep it running. I know there's none in town.'

'Probably up on the farms,' says Rose. 'They all had their own tanks, mostly diesel for the tractors, but they would've had another storage for running the farm bikes.'

'The hayshed!'

'What about it?'

'There were red containers up there. Jerry cans. That must be where they're storing it. If I can get to them, they'll have no fuel to run it.'

This is about as much as Rose has energy for. I help her up and get her back to the bedroom where she crawls under the blanket.

'I'll wake you when the soup's ready,' I say, though I'm sure she's already asleep.

Sometimes decisions are made for you. All you have to do is find the best way forward, and right now that's the least dangerous way of dealing with a dangerous situation.

I know that I have to get up to the hayshed as quick as I can, before they have the chance to refuel. But first I need to get my bike from our old place. I'm not going to risk moving out in the open while it's light, so I'll have to wait until tonight.

Over the next few hours, while Rose sleeps, I set up the place so she can get by here on her own—bring food in from the store, pump water into the header tank and make sure the gas bottle is full.

I need to get my stuff ready, too. The backpack with some supplies, matches, a knife, cans of beans, a map, some rope and a sleeping bag. It'll be a lot to carry on the bike, but I'll just have to find a way.

I've been so busy I've almost forgotten about the chicken. I break up the meat into the stock and add a little bit more salt and pepper. It will be easier for Rose to drink it so I ladle it into a cup and take it into her.

'You know how to keep a girl waiting,' she says, grinning. 'I've been lying here smelling that chicken for hours.'

She sits up in the bed, plumping the pillow behind her.

'I still can't believe it,' she says. 'Real chicken.'

I want to joke with her again, but I'm too preoccupied with what I need to do.

'So, what's the plan?' she says, between mouthfuls.

I try to keep it simple. I want her to believe it's possible. To be honest, I need to believe it's possible too.

'I'm going to get my bike soon and bring it back here. I'm packed and ready to go, so I'll check out the Wilders camp first then ride up to the hayshed.'

I take a big breath here because this is where it gets risky.

'I need to get them to follow me—to have them think we're both trying to escape north—so they'll abandon their camp and try to track us. I'll sleep up near the hayshed and in the morning I'm going to set it on fire, petrol and all. They'll see the smoke and come running.'

I stop there to see her reaction. Her eyes widen but, whether it's the fever, or tiredness, or even that she sees it's a good idea, she just nods and goes back to sipping at her soup.

'As soon as I've lit the place up I'll ride towards Pinchgut Junction. There's no guarantee they'll follow, but I'm hoping they'll head that way too because they'll need to find more fuel. They might leave someone here to guard their camp so you'll have to be careful. Stay inside. I'm going to leave Rowdy with you. He'll warn you if there's trouble. I've got no idea how long I'll be gone so I've drawn you a map to Ray's place. It's hidden under the sink, in the old flour tin. Keep it safe and destroy it when you've used it. I'm leaving you the bow and arrows, too. If I'm not back in a week and you're well enough, go out to Ray's and stay there with him. There's food in the kitchen and some honey from Ray. Mix it with hot water. Keep taking the antibiotics and change the bandage every day. I've torn up a sheet and the pieces are in the lounge room on the chair.'

I stop to draw breath and to give her time to say something, anything, to convince me it's not the stupidest plan she's ever heard. She's almost finished her soup and I can see a little bit of colour returning to her cheeks.

'I don't deserve this, Finn.'

'You deserve a chance,' I say. 'I always worried about Wilders coming and changing everything, but I never thought there'd be someone else on my side—someone I'd want to fight for.'

I've said more than I meant to and it sounds like something out of a war movie. But she sits back against the pillow and looks straight at me.

The afternoon is fading and the light in the room is dropping away. She slides to the side of the bed and pats the blanket for me to sit next to her.

'Stay with me for a few minutes,' she says. 'Until it gets dark. Until you have to go.'

I prop myself against the bedhead and we sit there with just our shoulders touching. I can feel the warmth of her through my shirt.

'What was it like for you, Finn? When your parents died?'

This isn't what I was expecting. I thought she'd want to hear more about the plan. How I would go about finding Kas. Outrunning the Wilders. The danger of it all.

'When Dad died,' I say at last, 'I still had Mum, and I felt like I'd be safe. I didn't realise how hard it must've been for her. We had no support in the town; it was dog-eat-dog by then. So we just threw ourselves into surviving, neither of us owning up to the big hole Dad had left in our lives. But when I lost Mum too, it was like time stopped. Even the simplest things were hard—like breathing. For weeks after that it was as though the world had tipped a little bit and everything was out of balance. I stumbled around trying to do things I'd been doing for years, but I just couldn't find a way through them. I guess I gave up.'

'But you made it through.'

'It was Ray. Just having that contact with someone again, someone to talk to. Funniest thing?'

'What?'

'The whole time, he never said anything about the way I talk—growly.'

She nudges me then, just being playful. And I nudge her back.

'You're still a bit hard to understand, dog boy, but I'm getting used to it.'

The light's dropped away altogether now and we sit in the dark of the room. I'm almost drifting off to sleep myself when she nudges me again.

'Hey,' she says. 'You awake?'

'Yep. Just.'

'I think your plan might work.'

Then, quietly in the dark, I feel her moving closer to me. She nuzzles into my neck. After a couple of minutes I feel a slight tremor go through her body and she sits up.

'Feel this,' she says, excited.

She presses my hand against her belly, but I don't feel anything.

'Wait,' she says.

And then, there it is, kicking. The baby.

Everything tonight is fizzing and cartwheeling—it's like there's too much to take in. Everything has been happening slowly for two years and now it's like time is going twice as fast, spinning and sliding out of control. I'm struggling to keep up.

'I can't do this on my own, Finn,' she says. 'You have to come back safely, okay? And you have to bring Kas.'

She lies back down with her head against my chest. We sit like this for ages until she pulls away.

'You won't save the world sitting here, dog boy,' she says.

'It's just us I'm trying to save. The world can look after

itself.' I slide off the bed and make my way back to the kitchen.

She calls from her room, 'Hey, any more of that soup going?'

After I've fetched her another cup of soup, I'm out the back door, careful to make sure Rowdy doesn't slip through and follow me. I keep to the shadows and make my way down the street towards the river to check on the Wilders.

I can see the glow of their campfire before I'm halfway there. Edging closer, I make out the shapes of six men, standing around the fire with their hands held out to the flames. To the left of them the light dances off the metal of the trailbike. I'm pretty sure they are all there so I head back up the street and walk parallel to the main road until I get to the bridge. Just as I'm about to break cover I notice a shape sitting with its back to the railings, midway across.

They're guarding the bridge.

'*Fuck*,' I breathe.

I should have expected this. It means I have to go further upriver to the footbridge. I back away and follow the trail along the bank to the old kids playground with its rusted swings and the seesaw angling into the sky. They built the footbridge when I was about ten, to encourage more kids to walk to school from this side of town. In summer we dived off it into the muddy water, knowing exactly where it was deep enough. I check it out in the moonlight for a good ten minutes before I make a move. There's no sign of it being watched so I cross quickly. From here, I run up the hill and cut through to the back lane that leads to our old house.

For that first year after Mum died, I used to come back here now and then to visit Dad's grave. But the memories became too much to cope with, haunting.

The door to the shed is rusty on its hinges. Dad would never have allowed that to happen. When I force it open and pull the torch from my back pocket, it's like everything inside has been frozen in time, with only a few cobwebs to show how long it's been since anyone came in here.

My mountain bike is where I left it, wedged in behind the foldaway table-tennis table. I'm pretty sure there are no punctures since the tyres aren't fully flat. Shining the torch around sends a stab of pain right through me. Dad was a stickler for keeping the shed neat and tidy and the whole side wall is marked with the outlines of saws and hammers and chisels and screwdrivers. None of the actual tools are left—they were stolen early on—but the outlines are like their ghosts, as though someone has been using them on a building project and forgotten to put them back. The sight of the empty wall hits me harder than I can put into words. It's about Dad and me and everything we had before the virus.

I find the pump on the floor. With the tyres holding air, I rustle around under the bench and find an old oilcan, one of those ones with the small plunger for your finger and a long nozzle. It's perfect for oiling the chain and gears. Then I wheel the bike into the yard and scooter out to the road.

Riding the bike again feels good. I realise I haven't moved this fast for ages—maybe surfing on a big day, but not on land. In a couple of minutes I'm back over the footbridge and following the river track. I slow down to check the sentry on the road bridge then turn further inland to wind my way back home.

I'm barely in the back door when I hear Rose call me. I flick on the torch and see she's sitting up, the empty soup cup on the bedside table.

'I've thought of something,' she says. She's got the leather strap with the ring attached wound around her fingers. 'Take this. Kas will recognise it. It will help her to trust you when you find her.'

She loops it over my head, then puts her hand over the ring and pushes the cool metal into my chest.

Out in the kitchen, I put the backpack on to check its weight, then ease it off onto the table. Rowdy gets up and starts leaping against the back door. I bend down and cup his face in my hands.

'Sorry, old boy, you have to stay here and look after Rose. She needs you.'

Then I go back to say goodbye to Rose.

'Don't turn on the torch,' she says as I stand in the doorway. So I have to try to picture her sitting there, the blanket hugged up around her chest and her hair falling over her face. It seems there's nothing to say that we haven't said already, and I listen to the silence.

'Go,' she says.

And without a word I turn back down the hallway, through the kitchen and out into the yard. I pull the backpack on, get on my bike and ride out onto the street.

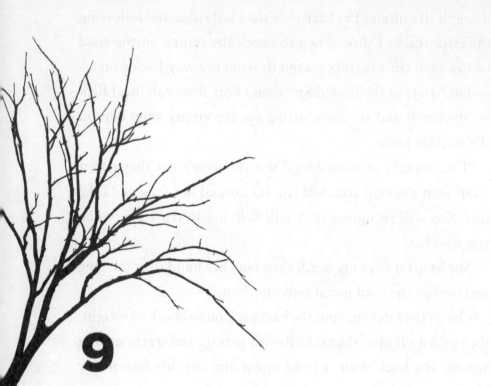

9

By the time I cross back over the footbridge, the clouds have
cleared and the moon is bright enough to cast a shadow. I
follow the track along the opposite bank of the river.

Within an hour, I'm lying low in the last of the bush before
it meets the farmland, checking the hayshed for any sign of life.
It all seems quiet. I need to ride parallel to the fence for a few
hundred metres to the gate by the corner of the paddock. It's
open. There's been no stock in there for ages, most killed by
hunters in the early days, and the rest gone feral in the bush.

At the gate, my tyres drop into the wider wheel tracks made
by the trailbike. This must be where Ramage rides in and out.

I'm halfway to the hayshed when the idea hits me. If I set fire to the shed, Ramage is likely to come ahead of the others on the trailbike to investigate. He'll come through that gate in a hurry, looking over at the burning shed...

I head back to the gate, risking turning the torch on to have a good look around. The tyre tracks are deep and spread wide, as though he has accelerated through. I walk along the fence looking for any loose wire.

It takes me a while, but eventually I find a length that's been broken at one end by a branch falling across it. I trace it back to the nearest post and start to work it up and down to break it.

The wire is hot in my hands but it soon comes free. I reckon it must be about five or six metres long—enough to stretch across the open gate at chest height. This is all eating up time when I should be sleeping. I'm going to need all my energy tomorrow to outrun the Wilders, but within half an hour I've tensioned off the wire on both sides of the gateposts. My hope is that Ramage won't see it and will hit it at speed. I'm not sure what I'll do then, but if I get to the trailbike I can do some damage to it.

By the time I'm bedded down in the hayshed the moon has set and the night has enveloped the paddock. I struggle to get to sleep—the plan keeps running over and over in my head—but eventually I drop off.

At first light, I start to get organised by riding my bike out along the track towards the road heading to Pinchgut Junction.

I hide it in the bush, marking its position by the hanging branch of a wattle.

Back in the shed I break open a few bales to loosen the hay. Then I drag a couple of dead branches out of the bush to keep the fire burning once the hay gets going. Finally, I empty the jerry cans over the top and I'm ready to put a match to it. The sun's been up for a good hour; I don't have time to waste. Still, I take a minute to rehearse the plan in my head one more time, knowing that once I light up the shed there'll be no going back. Then I strike the match, flick it from a distance and run.

The petrol makes the whole thing explode with a loud *whoomp*, and by the time I'm in my hiding place by the gate the fire has taken hold. I hadn't realised how quickly it would burn. The smoke plume, darkened by the burning petrol, rises well above the tree line and the northerly blows it down towards the coast. The flames take hold of the walls and roof, leaping wildly into the sky. I just hope the Wilders see it and panic.

It burns fast; the whole shed is consumed in about twenty minutes. Luckily, it keeps smoking even after the flames die down.

I'm not sure I actually hear it at first; the muffled noise of the trailbike is almost swamped by the sound of the wind and the final collapse of the shed's frame. But I pick it up again, louder this time and coming fast.

I bury myself in the low bracken and hold my breath. As I'd hoped, Ramage has come up from town the same way I did last night, straight up to the ridge and along the fence. He's in a rush too, throttling along, his head turned to the burning shed. It's hard to judge his speed, but by the time he swings into the gateway he must be doing at least thirty or forty. He hasn't seen the wire.

He hits it with force and his body seems to prop in mid-air while the trailbike lurches and continues on for a few metres before falling on its side and stalling. Ramage lands on the ground with a thud and an eerie quiet falls across the paddock. All I can hear is the hissing of the exhaust pipe against the wet grass.

Ramage stays on his back, but I can see his hands moving as he tries to work out what has happened. I have to hit my legs to get them moving, jumping up and running towards the trailbike.

Ramage has rolled onto his side, but he's still too stunned to stand up. The bike is lying on its side. I take the knife from my pocket and start cutting into the hoses running along the side of the motor, hoping one of them is the fuel line. Eventually petrol starts to spurt out of one. My breath is coming in bursts and I'm gulping for air. My hands are shaking and I feel like throwing up.

As I walk back past Ramage his eyes follow me. He tries to put out his hand to grab my leg, but there's no strength in the movement.

After everything Rose has told me, it's strange to see him up close. I've only ever seen him from a distance, on the day Rose arrived and then again when he speared the man on the ground over next to the hayshed. He doesn't look as rough as the other Wilders I've seen. His hair is cut shorter and his beard is more straggly than bushy. It's hard to guess his age with the dirt and blood covering his face, but I reckon he'd be forty, maybe fifty. Even with him lying on the ground, I can tell he's tall, six foot six, at least. He brings a hand to his face and smears blood from his forehead down his cheek and into his beard. Then he lifts the hand to his eyes. He focuses on me again and smiles a twisted smile.

'Fucker!' he spits between bloodstained teeth. 'I'll kill you, so help me God, I'll kill you.'

But he's vulnerable and he knows it. With my hands shaking even more now, I feel for the knife in my pocket again. I struggle to flick the blade into position. Before I realise what I'm doing, I've knelt down next to him and I'm holding the knife at his throat.

Everything up until now has been like a Boys' Own adventure story I could have read when I was a kid—the clever boy outsmarting the bad guys and saving the girl. But this is real, this holding a blade at a man's throat and looking him in the face. His eyes are opening and closing and there's blood gurgling in his throat as he tries to breathe. I know I can kill him with just a bit of pressure on the knife, but even though I feel that he doesn't deserve to live I can't bring myself to do it. Maybe it's Dad telling me there's always something good in everyone, or maybe it's something deep inside *me* that makes the decision.

Despite all of that, I still want to show him we're not afraid to fight back against him. I pick up his left wrist, turn his hand over and, looking away so I can't see the damage it does, I draw the knife across the back of his hand.

I'm shaking all over, dribbling snot everywhere and trying to form the words in my mouth.

Finally I say, 'That's for Rose, you bastard.'

I drop his hand back onto the dirt, roll him onto his side to stop him choking and run off towards my bike.

Loud enough for him to hear, I call, 'Grab the gear, Rose, we gotta head north before the others get here.'

I retrieve my backpack from the bracken and start running along the track to where I've hidden the bike. My legs are like jelly, but soon I'm pushing my way along the track that leads to the road north.

Once I hit the road I make good time. The wind has picked up again but the sun is out and there's no sign of rain. The bitumen surface is still pretty good, with only a few fallen branches blocking my way. I ride as hard as I can for about an hour before pulling to the side of the road, where I fall off and lie like a stranded turtle flipped on its back.

I reckon I'm about fifteen kilometres from the hayshed, which gives me a good three-hour headstart on the Wilders. Even then, Ramage will be slowing them down, if they haven't finished him off themselves. They could just abandon him there and try to track me without him.

I haven't eaten anything since I left Rose last night so I open the backpack and find the piece of chicken I pulled out of the pot before I headed off. I tear it in half and save the rest for later. It's dry and tough, but I don't think I've ever tasted anything so good. The smell of it reminds me of Rose, sitting up in the bed with her hands wrapped around the cup of soup.

The warm wind and the sun on my skin bring me back to the roadside. It's time to get moving. It's still only mid-morning so I can make it to Pinchgut Junction before sundown if I hurry.

Before long, the road is too steep for me to ride. I decide to leave the bike, hide it by the side of the road and continue on foot. Up ahead, in a paddock to the right of the road, I see an old windmill next to a rusted-out tank. I stash the bike behind the tank and heave the pack onto my back again.

It feels strange to be walking at such a slow pace after the events of the morning. My legs are heavy now that all the excitement has settled down, but the sun is out and it's almost peaceful. I have to be on my guard against danger—and maybe not just from the Wilders behind me. It's likely they've left someone to guard the junction, keeping an eye on movements along the road. All I've done so far is buy myself time by damaging the trailbike and injuring Ramage. They'll still be coming after me and I've got no real idea how to go about finding Kas.

My hope is that she won't have strayed too far from the road, that she'll be watching for any sign of her sister coming back for her. Or that she'll be making her way to the coast.

Every few hundred metres I stop and listen, looking up and down the road for movement. But the afternoon passes and I find myself gradually climbing towards the junction by sunset. It's almost dark by the time I get up to the top of the cutting where I can look down at the road.

And, sure enough, there's the glimmer of a fire below me. I decide to bed down for the night and check them out in the morning. I find some bracken fern that I can pull up and make a sort of bed. My stomach is calling out for food, but I can't risk a fire, so I open a can of beans and eat them cold before climbing into my sleeping bag, pulling the pack under my head for a pillow and collapsing into sleep.

10

Sometimes it's hard to pick the difference between a bad dream and reality, but I know I'm fully awake when I feel the weight of a man sitting on top of me, his hand over my mouth. My arms are trapped inside the sleeping bag so there's nothing I can do to defend myself. His face is so close to mine I can smell his stinking breath.

'Not a word, boyo. Not a word!' he whispers.

As my eyes adjust to the dark, I can make out two other figures. The one that's been sitting on me pulls me to my feet and ties a gag around my mouth. He lifts me out of the sleeping bag so the third man can stuff it into the backpack. My hands are tied behind my back and my boots shoved onto my feet, and then we're on the move.

I stumble and trip, but a rope has been tied to my wrists and I'm pulled back up each time I fall. I'm shit-scared but still alert enough to realise we're moving north.

We walk for what seems like hours. I've fallen over so many times I can feel blood running down into my boots from my knees. The first light of morning is creeping through the trees when we make our way out onto the road again. With the sun beginning to rise off to my right I realise we're heading towards Swan's Marsh. I hope this isn't the group that tried to capture Rose when she came through a few days ago. If it is, they'll hand me over to Ramage, for sure.

Eventually they slow down and the leader says, 'We'll take a break here. Five minutes. No more.'

I'm dragged to the side of the road and pushed down until I'm sitting. The leader leans over me and releases the gag, but he doesn't untie my wrists.

'Sorry, laddie,' he says. 'We couldn't take any chances. There were men guarding the junction. I guess you saw them or you wouldn't have been up where you were.'

His voice is different now, less aggressive, almost friendly. But I'm still on my guard.

'Who are you and where are you from?' I ask.

The three of them laugh.

'What kinda language is that?' says the leader. 'You sound like a wild animal. And I reckon we'll be the ones asking the questions.'

I slow right down and try to make the words come out without growling.

'Name's Finn. I've been living rough just the other side of the junction.'

'Yeah, and I'm Jesus Christ and these are my apostles,' says the man, pointing at the other two.

They all fall about laughing like this is the funniest thing they've ever heard.

'You haven't been living rough, not by the look of you. You've had a roof over your head, I reckon. And that sleeping bag hasn't been out in the weather, either.'

His voice is more serious now.

'Personally,' he says, 'I don't give a rat's arse where you've come from, long as there's no Wilders following you.'

I stay quiet.

'These parts there are bands of Wilders on the lookout for anyone of use to them. Women, in particular. They work out of Longley. Rough mob.'

'Ramage,' I say, and they all turn to look at me at once.

'What'd you know about Ramage?' the leader says.

'I know what he does.'

He stands over me, trying to figure me out. 'If you're on the run, you're travelling in the wrong direction,' he says. 'You're heading *towards* Longley. Want to tell us exactly what you're up to, boy?'

It sounds like they're against Ramage, but that doesn't mean they aren't as bad—or worse—than him. But I don't feel threatened. There's something about the leader that makes me want to trust him.

'Got any food?' I ask. 'I'm starving.'

They look at each other and leader nods. One of the other two rummages in his bag and pulls out what looks like a piece of bread. I have to blink to make sure I'm not imagining it.

'Bread?' I can't believe it.

He breaks off a piece and tries to hand it to me before he realises my hands are still tied behind my back.

'Untie him,' the leader says. 'Let him eat.'

The tall, thickset man with long hair and a scraggly beard unties me and hands me the bread. I tear at it like I haven't eaten in months. It's strange; it's not the taste that hits me first, it's the texture, something I haven't felt for so long I've forgotten it. The way it kind of breaks down into that grainy feel in my mouth. Then the taste kicks in and I have this flood of memories about school lunches and toast and crusty bread from the bakery on Saturday mornings.

'Ease up, eat slow. You'll make yourself sick.'

'Sorry,' I say, spraying crumbs out onto the ground. 'It's been a while.'

They're still eyeing me, but I sense they are relaxing.

The man in charge starts talking again. 'I'm Harry, and this is Tusker and Jack.'

Tusker is the big bloke that untied me and Jack is smaller and thinner, but wiry. Strong.

'So you're not Jesus, then,' I say and they all laugh again.

'Funny bastard,' says Tusker. When he turns into the sun I notice a scar that runs from his forehead down across his left eye to his cheek, where it disappears into his beard. The eye is partly closed.

'You lot with Ramage or against him?' I ask.

'We got nothing to do with Ramage,' Tusker says. 'We stay clear of him. Given the chance, though, I'd tie the bastard up to a tree and shoot him through the heart. If he had one.'

I have to be careful what I reveal, but I need these men to help me.

'I saw him yesterday,' I say.

'Who'd you see?'

'Ramage.'

'Where?' Harry says.

I shrug. 'South.'

'He on his trailbike?'

'Kinda.'

'What'd ya mean, kinda?'

'He met with a bit of an accident.'

Tusker shakes his head and spits.

'What sort of an accident?' Harry says.

They're leaning in towards me now. I give them a rough account of what happened, but I limit the detail: nothing about Rose or Angowrie. When I finish they lean back and I can see they're trying to figure out whether I'm telling the truth or not.

Tusker speaks first. 'Well, ain't you full of surprises. I don't know if what you just told us is complete bullshit, but I hope to Christ it's not. If it's true there'll be a lot of people who'd like to thank you. Ramage is a dangerous bastard—kill you just for the fun of it.'

Jack speaks for the first time then. His voice is low and deep. 'How many men with him?'

'Four or five. I reckon they'll be tracking me. If Ramage can travel.'

'They'll get word to those blokes at the junction soon enough,' Harry says. 'We'd better get moving. We'll stay off the road.'

'What do we do with him,' Tusker says, pointing at me.

'Sorry, young fella,' Harry says, 'but we travel light. And we got no extra food. I wish you the best of luck.' He puts out his hand for me to shake.

'Which way are you going?'

I'm taking a chance here but I don't have much option.

'You're still not making sense to us, boy,' Jack says. 'You haven't explained why you're travellin' north. Ramage is behind you and you're heading further into his country. Doesn't figure.'

'I'm looking for someone,' I say. 'A girl.'

Harry turns and walks over to where I'm standing by the side of the road.

'We're all looking for girls,' he says. 'But Finn, there's hardly any women left, you know that, yeah?'

'I know. But this girl's alive. At least, she was a few days ago.'

'How do you know?'

'A friend saw her.'

'A friend? Where?'

'Near Swan's Marsh.'

Tusker and Jack come over and the three of them stand in a semicircle around me. The sun's behind them and they cast long shadows.

It'd be hopeless trying to look for Kas on my own. I don't know the country this side of the range and she could be anywhere. I have to take the chance that these men know something.

Tusker says, 'Swan's Marsh is no place for a girl. The Monahan clan live there and they take their orders from Ramage.'

'She was escaping from them,' I say. 'She was on horseback. Her name's Kas. She's got a birthmark on her face.'

I've got their attention now. The other two look to Harry, expecting him to make a decision.

'What're you thinking?' he says to Tusker.

'Dunno. He just appears out of nowhere. Tells us some story about Ramage. He could be working for him, for all we know. Could be leading Ramage right to us—'

Jack interrupts. 'Scrawny little prick. Dunno how he's stayed alive for so long. He's got to have been living somewhere. Someone older looking after him.'

I'm losing them.

'Been holed up on the coast,' I say. 'In an old shack. Living off rabbits, fish, crays, anything I can catch. I wouldn't slow you down and I'm a good hunter. I'm not with Ramage. I hate him.'

I try really hard to hold them back, but tears have started to run down my face.

Everything seems to go quiet then; the wind drops away like it's holding its breath.

'All right, listen up,' says Harry. 'You can come with us, but we're going to have to blindfold you. We've got a place. It's a good day's walk from here and there's some rough country in between.'

Tusker's not happy. He swears under his breath and spits again. 'I'm not dragging him,' he says.

'Me neither,' says Jack.

'I'll lead him,' Harry says. There's a solidness about him that reminds me of Dad. He leans in and ties a rag around my head, covering my eyes.

'Not too tight?' he says. Then I feel the rope around my wrists again, but in front this time. There's a gentle tug and we're on our way.

The first hour or so isn't too bad. We're still on the road. I can feel the even surface under my feet and we move at a good pace. No one is saying much, but every now and again Harry asks how I'm going. Tusker and Jack have either dropped back behind us or they're out in front, maybe scouting for danger. I can't hear their footsteps.

Harry starts talking low, like he doesn't want the others to hear. 'How do you know this girl, this Kas?' he asks.

If he is anything like my dad, he'll be able to tell when I'm lying, so I need to stick pretty close to the truth without giving too much away.

'Her brother turned up on the coast a few days ago,' I say. 'He was being chased by Wilders.'

'Her brother?'

'Yeah. Tom. He'd done something to them back in Longley and they tracked him to the coast.'

'I thought there was no one down there—on the coast, I mean.'

'There's not. It was quarantined early on.'

'You got family?'

'Had. All dead,' I say. 'Dad went first, then Mum. Got no brothers or sisters.'

'And you've survived how long?'

'I dunno. Maybe two years.'

'That's pretty right. We've been trying to keep track of time, but the seasons aren't what they used to be. Long summers. Wild winters.'

We've fallen into an easy conversation, but I know he's still trying to suss me out.

'The coast's changed too,' I say. 'The king tides come right up and flood the rivers and swamps.'

Harry goes quiet. Maybe he suspects I'm not telling him everything.

'This fella, Tom,' he says after a while, 'where is he now?'

'Down on the coast. He didn't want to travel north again.'

'So why are you so keen to find his sister?'

I'm painting myself into a corner. I have to think fast.

'He saved my life,' I say. 'Saved me from Ramage.'

'So now you have to find his sister? Is she on the run from Ramage too?'

'I guess so.'

'Strange that Ramage would worry about a boy and not go after the girl.'

I can tell he's getting more and more suspicious. But just as I'm trying to work out what to say next, I hear a sharp whistle and Harry pulls me off the side of the road into the bush. He's got his hand in my back and he's pushing me down onto the ground.

'Stay quiet,' he says, urgent.

I hear heavy, shuffling footsteps and the squeaking of wheels. Low voices. Harry breathing, close to my ear. We stay down as the voices gradually drop away.

'Drifters,' he says. 'There's still a few of them on the roads. Just men and boys. There were only five in that group. Looked half starved and edgy. There's nothing we can do for them.'

There's shuffling in the bush behind us and I hear two heavy bodies drop to the ground. I recognise Tusker's voice.

'We'll never get there pulling this kid blind,' he snarls.

'Nearly time to leave the road anyway,' Harry says. 'We'll wait here till dark, then move on.'

Harry takes off the blindfold and undoes the rope around my wrists. Tusker and Jack move off on their own, not quite out of hearing range. Harry passes me my backpack. I open it, pull out the last of the chicken and offer him a small piece.

'Bloody hell, boyo,' he says. 'Chicken!'

I'm working hard to keep him onside. I feel safer with him than the other two. The sun is low in the sky now so I know we won't be resting for long.

Harry sits with his back against a fallen log and stretches out his legs. It's the first chance I've had to really look at him. I guess he must be about forty, but living rough can age a man quickly. He has a long face, a high forehead and thinning hair. His clothes are well looked after, no holes or split seams. When he eases his boots off I see his socks have been darned. He's either a good sewer or he knows someone who is.

'You got kids, Harry?' I ask.

'Yep. A girl, Willow.'

'She okay? Survived the virus, I mean?'

He glances towards the others and says, 'I had two. Another girl. Holly. She passed away early on.'

When he turns back to me I can see the hurt just saying that brought to his face.

'And I'm sorry about your mum and dad, son,' Harry says, his voice softer. 'It's been tough all over. Families broken up and kids left on their own. Most have died, I reckon. You've done a bloody good job just to stay alive.'

Then he says, 'I know you're probably not telling us everything, but it pays to play your cards close to your chest these days. Anyhow,' he adds, 'you'd best get some kip. We've got a long night ahead of us.'

He picks his hat up and covers his face, and I know the conversation is over. I lie back into the bracken and close my eyes.

11

It feels like I've only been asleep a couple of minutes when someone kicks my boot. I wake with a start and look up through the trees to the night sky. There's a half-moon and it casts just enough light to see through the bush.

'Come on, we're moving,' says Harry.

Tusker and Jack are already ahead of us, two dark shapes weaving their way between the trees.

'No blindfold now, son. Just try to keep up,' Harry says before he turns his back and takes off. My pack has been left for me to carry so I lift it onto my back and follow.

It's pretty easy going, at first. We stay on the flat mostly, trying to avoid the mimosa bushes that tear at our skin. The forest is different from the southern side of the ridge, taller, with more manna gums and thinner undergrowth.

I manage the pace, even though the pack is awkward to carry in the rougher terrain. I try to note landmarks along the way, rock outcrops on the ridge above or a particular fallen tree, but after a while I give up. I'd struggle to find my way back to the road.

After two hours or so, the moon is higher and the forest has become thicker. The gullies are filled with fern trees too dense to get through, so we have to climb up and around each one as we come to them. I can hear the trickle of water hidden deep in the ferns. The ground is wetter, too, and I lose my footing a couple of times. Only Harry shows any concern, calling a couple of times to ask if I'm okay.

The moon eventually drops behind us and the forest darkens again. We've moved higher. The air is cooler and low clouds scud just above the treetops. A light rain starts to fall, enough to wet my clothes through to the skin. The pack's getting heavier and my boots struggle to grip the damp forest floor. Without the moonlight I trip more regularly and my clothes are caked in mud. I lose all track of time, concentrating on putting one foot in front of the other.

Ahead I hear Harry's voice. 'Not long now, son.'

That encouragement is all I need to keep going until the sky starts to lighten and the misty rain eases. We've started to head downhill. Every now and again I get a glimpse of an open valley below and it spurs me on. Anything to be out of the trees, anything to lie down and rest.

As the forest starts to thin and the valley draws closer I pick up the smell of smoke. I catch up to the other three, and they seem more relaxed now, striding out and talking among themselves.

Harry drops back and we walk side by side for a few minutes.

'We've been here two years,' he says without looking at me, 'keeping ourselves out of sight. There are fifteen of us. We grow most of what we need—wheat, barley, fodder for the cattle. The valley's cut off by the range at the high end and there's a narrow entrance where the river cuts through at the other. We hunt up in the high country for strays gone wild and there's always plenty of rabbits.'

When we drop below the tree line, the whole valley opens up in front of us. There are four houses and a cluster of outbuildings. Smoke drifts from the chimney of the nearest house and I can see people moving about between the sheds.

Harry cups his hands in front of his mouth and blows long and slow, like the hooting of an owl. Two figures, one tall and one short, appear on the verandah of the house with the smoking chimney. The smaller one starts running towards us. Harry chuckles.

As the figure draws closer I see it's a girl, blonde-haired, maybe seven or eight years old. She gets within twenty metres and stops, looking at me, then at Harry.

'It's okay, Wils,' he says. 'He won't hurt you.'

125

The girl runs to Harry, and he scoops her up and throws her over his shoulder. She squeals and wraps her arms around his neck.

'Who's that, Daddy?'

'Just a stray we picked up,' Harry says, smiling.

The girl drops to the ground and circles me warily. She looks healthy, well fed. Her skin is clear and her hair is tied with a ribbon. Like her father's, her clothes are well cared for.

'Hello,' I say and she laughs.

'He talks funny. Why does he talk funny?'

'Finn's been on his own for a while. Come on,' Harry says, 'I'm hungry.'

He leads us down the hill. Tusker and Jack have already disappeared into one of the other houses. The girl darts in and out of her father's legs, looking at me every now and again, still uncertain.

'What's your name?' I ask, which makes her laugh again.

But when Harry gives her a stern look, she says, 'My name's Willow, and I'm eight.'

'My name's Finn,' I say, 'and I'm sixteen—I think.'

People have begun to appear out the front of the first house, crowding onto the verandah. Jack and Tusker stand with their arms folded across their chests. I count another eight people, adults and children. At least two of them are girls, and there's a woman at the front drying her hands on the side of her jeans.

She's the first to talk and her voice reminds me of Mum's.

'Well, well,' she says. 'Look what the cat dragged in.'

She walks around me, checking me from every angle.

'You certain about him?' she says to Harry.

'He's got no signs of the virus, Stell. He's made of pretty tough stuff, I reckon. Been on his own for two winters down on the coast. It didn't seem right to leave him out there, not with Ramage on the hunt.'

Tusker and Jack must have told the others what had happened.

'He needs a haircut and a good wash,' the woman says, with a small smile. 'Scrawny bugger. What have you got to say for yourself, young man?'

I don't know what to say. I'm embarrassed with everyone looking at me and I'm afraid they'll laugh when they hear my voice. I look at the ground and run my hand back through my hair.

'All right, everyone,' Harry says. 'Go easy on the boy. No need to interrogate him just yet. We need a good feed. Let's get inside. The rest of you, back to work. We'll have a meeting tonight.'

They all head off towards the other houses, though a couple of the younger ones look back over their shoulders, checking me out. Willow stands next to me, looking up.

'You're tall,' she says.

'You're short,' I say.

'We got porridge,' she says and skips to the door.

I look back at Harry. The woman is hugging him, her feet almost lifting off the ground in her effort to get her arms around his neck. He winks at me and says, 'Hungry, Finn?'

Inside, the house is warm and dry. It has that lived-in feel that family homes have, with cushions on a long couch, photos on the walls and something I haven't seen in years—Lego strewn across the lounge room floor.

There's a wood stove in the kitchen with a bubbling pot on top. Stella spoons porridge into two bowls and the steam rises to her face. Harry nods towards a chair at the kitchen table and I sit down. Willow sits next to me.

'Do they call you Thin cos you're so skinny?' she asks.

'It's not *Thin*, it's *Finn*.' I laugh, drawing out the *F*.

The porridge is hot and sweet. I can taste milk in it. Mine's half gone before I realise no one else has started.

'We say grace here, Finn,' Stella says.

I put my spoon down quietly. Harry places his hand in Stella's and reaches across to hold mine. Next to me, Willow completes the circle.

'Lord,' says Harry, 'bless this food and those who share it. Guide us in these troubled times and keep us safe from privation. Amen.'

'Amen,' I say.

'We think it's important that we hold to our faith, especially now,' Stella says.

I can only nod. I think about the church people in Angowrie when the virus hit. They tried to help the sick, but they just got the disease themselves and died.

By the time I'm finished my porridge I'm so tired I can hardly hold the spoon. The long night has caught up with me and I'm thinking of sleep.

'There's a bed through that door there,' Harry says, pointing behind me. 'And the washroom is out the back. There'll only be cold water at such short notice, but Stella won't let you get between clean sheets without you having a good wash first. Once you've rested we'll work out what we're going to do with you. There's plenty of work to be done on the farm.'

I'm too tired to argue that I didn't come with Harry to be put to work on his farm. I need to find Kas and get back to Rose.

'There'll be a community meeting tonight where everyone has a vote,' he says. 'We're a collective here. Others will have their say, too.'

The washroom has a concrete floor and there is a trough with cold water and a bucket. I strip off, tip a bucket of water over my head and use some soap that's as hard as wax to wash myself. My legs and arms are covered with scratches, but I scrub myself clean and dab the cuts dry.

The kitchen is empty when I walk back through. The porridge bowls are stacked on the bench, and the shelves are lined with jars of dried flowers and herbs. I close my eyes and breathe in the smell of people, the smell of a home.

Harry wasn't joking: there are clean sheets on the bed. I feel a bit guilty, but I slide in and my head barely hits the pillow before I'm asleep.

The day is almost over when I wake. There are fresh clothes hanging on the end of the bed. They're a bit big for me, but at least they're dry.

Outside, the sun has dropped below the ridge to the west and the whole valley is in shadow. There are three figures walking up to the house, tools carried across their shoulders. They're too far away to make out, but I guess one of them is Harry from his height and the way he walks. As they draw closer the other two peel off towards the sheds. Harry leans his tools, a hoe and an axe, on the side of the verandah and comes inside.

'We'd best be getting ready for that meeting, son,' he says.

The meeting takes place in a communal hall lit by spirit lamps. There's an inner circle of six chairs and an outer one of ten. Half-a-dozen figures are already sitting in the inner circle. It takes a while for my eyes to adjust to the light, but slowly I make out five men and a woman, ranging in age from about fifteen to forty.

Harry sits in the inner circle. Stella guides me to a chair behind him then sits down next to Harry. Eventually the chairs fill—each person seems to have their own place, but it's too dark to see everyone properly.

Harry is the first to speak.

'May the Lord guide and direct us in our decisions tonight,' he says, 'and in His mercy help us to do what is right for our community.'

This is followed by a muffled 'Amen' from the others.

Harry leans forward in his chair and sits his palms flat on his thighs. He gets straight to the point.

'As you know, Jack Wilson, Peter Tusker and myself have spent the last couple of days in the forest. We travelled as far as the coast road at Pinchgut Junction, where we came across the boy, Finn. Stand up, lad,' he says.

I get to my feet and small conversations break out around the circle.

'Righto, righto,' Harry says. 'The lad says he's been living rough in the bush down by the coast and that he's on the run from Ramage and his men. He tells us he's looking for someone. A girl.'

Everyone laughs and I hear a deep voice call out, 'Aren't we all, aren't we all.'

Harry waves his hand and they fall silent. 'Anyways,' he says, 'we brought him back here because we can always do with an extra hand on the farm, if he chooses to stay. If he's survived on his own for this long, he must be pretty tough. And a good hunter. So,' he says, more seriously, 'we need to decide whether we welcome the boy into our community or let him go.'

This isn't what I was expecting.

Tusker is sitting in the inner circle, opposite Harry and Stella, and he waits for quiet before he speaks. The low light makes his scar look sinister, curling up his lip on one side. His eyes move around the group.

'It wasn't my idea to bring him back here,' he says. 'The boy's story doesn't add up. He says he's running from Ramage, but he's heading north. Says he's been living rough, but he doesn't look like he has. How do we know he ain't with Ramage, finding out where we are and leading him back here? I say we keep him here, under lock and key if we have to. The community comes first. We can't take risks.'

Harry's voice rises again. 'Finn says he had a run-in with Ramage before he left the coast. Says he nearly killed him. Knocked him off his trailbike. That's why he's being chased.'

'Sounds like bullshit to me. Just another story he's making up,' Tusker says.

'There's something else he's told me.' Harry pauses before going on. 'Finn claims there's another boy down on the coast who's got a sister called Kas. Finn's trying to find her to take her back to her brother. The girl's got a birthmark on her face.'

This last bit of information kills all the sound in the room and everyone turns to the back row opposite me. A girl stands up, and as the light hits her face I see the red birthmark running down the left-hand side. Even in the dull light I can see her skin is as brown as Rose's. Her hair is pulled back and her eyes shine in the lamplight.

Harry speaks. His voice is deep, grave. 'Kashmala, do you know this boy? Have you ever seen him before?'

The girl clears her throat. 'No, I never seen him before. Not around Longley. And'—she pauses for effect—'I've got no brother.'

The room erupts again. I can hear Tusker's voice rising above the others.

'I told you,' he says, 'I told you he was a fuckin' liar.'

Harry waits for quiet again, then addresses Tusker. 'I'll ask you to mind your tongue.'

Tusker smirks and looks away.

Harry turns back to Kas and says, 'Are you sure, girl? Come over here and have a closer look at him.'

She walks slowly around the outer circle until she is next to me. While everyone is watching her, I slip the leather strap with the ring from around my neck and hide it in my hand.

Kas has the same dark eyes as Rose, but her face is leaner, longer, and she's a good six inches taller than her sister.

She shakes her head. 'No, I've never seen him before,' she says again. Her accent is as strong as Rose's.

It's darker over where I've been sitting so, while more anxious conversation breaks out around the room, I reach out and grab Kas by the wrists and push the ring into her palm. I'm close enough to see her eyes widen as she feels it in her hand, but she says nothing. I hold her gaze and give her the slightest of nods.

'All right, Kashmala, you can sit down again now,' Harry says. He looks at me like a disappointed father. 'Sit down, Finn,' he says, turning away.

Tusker is on his feet. The others are staring at him, seeming to urge him on.

'I dunno why we're even having this conversation, Harry. The girl's a Siley. She's got no rights. She's our property now. And if Ramage ever finds the valley we can use her to trade. The boy's lied to us from the start. We can't risk letting him go and him leading Ramage back here.'

The others nod and grunt in agreement.

'The lad's done nothing wrong,' says Harry above the noise of the room. 'I dunno why he's made up the story about the girl's brother, but he's seen her somewhere before. Otherwise how would he know about her birthmark?'

'Come on, Harry, think about it. We know the girl's a

133

runaway. This just proves the boy's working with Ramage. He's from Longley too, and he was heading back there when we caught him. I say we keep them both here and have them work alongside the rest of us.'

'They're no one's property, Tusker. They're God's children.'

'Not everyone here shares your faith, Harry,' says Tusker. 'I don't care whose children they are, they'll stay here and work and they'll feel my whip if they don't.'

The others are cheering and clapping now. As they push forward to pat Tusker on the back I get a clear view of Kas. Looking straight at me she brings her hand up to her face and I see the ring glint in the lamplight.

'It doesn't matter who they are, Tusker,' Harry says, 'we've got an obligation to treat them kindly. They're just kids. Where's your humanity?'

'I lost my humanity when my wife and kids died. Where was your merciful God then?'

'You know how sorry I am for your loss. I lost a daughter too.'

'Sorry, bullshit, Harry! You were lucky. You've got a wife to keep you warm at night. And another daughter.'

'You can't blame me for that,' Harry says.

'I'm not blaming you, but we're coming at this current situation from different angles. The girl's old enough to have children. That's about all Sileys are good for—that and working the fields. If they wanted otherwise they shouldn't've come to this country in the first place.'

Stella cuts in then. 'They were children, Tusker. Children!

They had no say in where their parents brought them.'

'More bullshit,' Tusker says. 'Besides, everyone knows they brought the virus.'

Stella sits up straight. I can feel her anger from here.

'There's never been any proof of that, Tusker, and you know it.'

'That's not worth wasting our breath on now. We got a problem here and we have to solve it. And we reckon,' he says, looking around the chairs on his side of the room, 'we reckon it's too dangerous to let the boy go.'

The others all nod in agreement and more noise breaks out around the room.

Harry whispers something to Stella before facing the others again.

'We've got no problem with them staying in the valley, but let them grow up, help work the farm and, when they're old enough, choose their own partners. Stella and I will take them in, we've got room.'

Harry's voice is measured. Calm. The younger men on Tusker's side seem to be swayed by his authority. But Tusker is shaking his head.

'Why should you take them in? You got a wife. You got a daughter. We don't have enough women here and we have to think about the future. Pity she's so ugly.'

The others around Tusker laugh and I feel the balance shift back to their side of the room.

But Tusker has barely finished his sentence when Kas launches from her seat. She's on his back in an instant, raining blows down on his head. Everyone seems to freeze, too stunned to move. Tusker is a big man and Kas's punches just glance off him. As he brings his arms up to grab her, she leans in close. He lets out a yelp and hurls her across the floor like a ragdoll. His hand goes to his ear and I can see blood trickling through his cupped fingers. He brings his hands to the front of his face.

'You fuckin' bitch,' he yells, jumping to his feet and standing over her. He raises his fist to hit her, but before he can land a punch two things happen at once. Harry grabs his raised arm and Kas directs a kick into his crotch. Tusker reels back in pain, as everyone in the room seems to dive into the heap of arms and legs and bodies.

I take hold of Kas's hand and drag her away from the fight. I think she might be unconscious, but once I get her to clear space behind where I was sitting she opens her eyes and stares at me.

'Where did you get the ring?' she whispers.

'From Rose.'

'Where is she?'

'She's safe,' I say, as slow and clear as I can. 'In Angowrie, down on the coast. I'm going back to her. Are you with me?'

She doesn't get the chance to answer. A big hand grabs her by the arm and drags her back to the other side of the room.

A couple of the older men have pulled the fighters apart and some calm descends on the room. A man I'd heard them call Simmo stands between the two groups, an arm outstretched to each.

'Righto, that'll do,' he says. 'Back off, everyone.'

People start taking their seats again. No one seems to be

hurt, apart from Tusker who has one hand between his legs rubbing his balls and the other trying to stem the flow of blood from his ear. I can see a flap of skin hanging off the top where Kas has bitten him.

'All right,' Simmo says. 'We all agree the boy and the Siley stay here in the valley. It's too much of a risk to let them go. Unless we want to lock them up, they need to stay with someone. I say we separate them. The boy can stay with Harry and Stella and the girl with Rachel and me.'

Everyone turns to the woman who's been sitting next to Kas through the meeting. She must be Rachel. It seems like there's agreement on this, going by the nodding heads and the grunts of approval.

Rachel takes Kas by the shoulders and marches her to the door. Kas swings around and looks right at me.

'Finn,' she calls across the room. 'The answer's yes.'

12

When the meeting breaks up, Harry, Stella and I walk back to the house. As we approach the door, Stella grabs me by the wrists.

'I want you to promise me something,' she says. 'When you walk through that door, when you enter our house, you don't tell us any more lies. It's the truth from now on, you hear?'

The last week has been such a jumble of half-truths and lies that I hardly know what's real and what's not anymore. But there's something binding in the way she looks at me.

'No more lies,' I say.

She nods at Harry, and the three of us go inside and sit down at the table.

'Now,' Harry says, 'you'd better give us the whole story, Finn.'

So I tell them about Rose and everything that has happened since she arrived in Angowrie. I watch their faces carefully while I talk, but they don't seem too surprised. Not until I tell them that Rose is pregnant.

Stella is excited and angry.

'She's pregnant?' she cries. 'And on her own surrounded by Ramage's mob? Why did you leave her down there?'

'I had no choice. If I hadn't gone, she would've gone herself. And that would've been even more dangerous. For her and the baby.'

Stella smiles. 'You've got a good head on your shoulders, Finn. Your mum and dad would be proud.'

I don't know what to say to this, but something warm glows inside me.

We all fall silent. They're both weighing up what to do, but I've made my decision. I made it the minute I saw Kas at the meeting. It's just a matter of whether Stella and Harry are going to help us or not.

'Tell me about when Kas arrived,' I say.

'She's been here a few days now,' Harry says. 'One of our young blokes, James, got separated on a hunting party last week. He found his way over towards Swan's Marsh and spotted the girl on her own. There was some sort of commotion going on in the town, and she took the chance to steal a horse and make off with it. James led her back here. To start with she was pretty happy just to have a feed and a roof over her head, but then she told us she had to leave.'

He hesitates, twisting the wedding ring on his finger.

'I'm sorry about what happened at the meeting, Finn. You didn't see us at our best. You probably worked out that Tusker has pretty different views from mine.'

I almost smile. 'Yeah, I picked that up.'

'Kashmala—Kas,' he corrects himself, 'has done a bit of work around the place, mostly on her horse. She doesn't let it out of her sight. Sleeps in the barn with it. When I saw her ride it, I understood why.'

Stella has been quiet but now she says, 'We're in a difficult situation, Finn. No one in the community is going to allow you to leave, especially not with Kas. But I can't bear to think of her sister down there on the coast fending for herself. Not with a baby coming.'

'There's no use trying to escape,' Harry adds. 'They all know this country better than you do. Tusker and Wilson are good bushmen, they'd catch you before you made it to Pinchgut Junction, drag you back here and lock you up.'

Stella leans across the table then and puts her hand on my arm.

'What if we could get Rose here, into the valley with us,' she says. 'She'd be safer—and so would her baby.'

'Being around the likes of Tusker doesn't feel very safe to me,' I say. 'Look at the way he treats Kas. He'll know straightaway that Rose is a Siley and that means her baby will be a Siley too.'

'You're not alone here, Finn,' Harry says. 'Stella and me will stick up for all of you. The most important thing is bringing that baby into the world safely. It's the best chance Rose's got.'

I'm tossing everything up in mind. Maybe they're right. I've got no idea what to do when the baby comes and I'm guessing Kas hasn't either. Ray might be able to help us, but even he admitted he doesn't know much about childbirth. Still, I don't trust anyone here apart from Harry and Stella. The others could take the baby and force Rose to work on the farm.

I tell them I need to sleep on it. I don't want to be rushed into another decision that leaves me up shit creek. I console myself with the fact that I'm still the only one here who knows exactly where Rose is, though I worry that she'll grow tired of waiting for me. If she does, I hope she has the sense to follow my directions to Ray's place.

The next few days pass quickly. Even though I'm edgy to leave, there's something satisfying about working on the farm. I stay close to Harry most of the time, hardly talking to anyone else. We work along the river, getting the paddocks ready for ploughing. The soil is soft and dark brown. Harry says it's good for cropping. There's capeweed and thistles in thin patches and we work at rooting them out.

Every now and then I scan the valley, looking at the other groups of workers for any sign of Kas. I think I see her once across the river, but I can't tell at such a distance. And my eyes are drawn to the steep country leading up to the ridge. It looks rugged and difficult to climb but, if we could find a way, it's the quickest way back to Pinchgut Junction.

At the end of the day the different work teams return to their own houses. When we get close to ours, Willow runs out to meet Harry. He sweeps her up and carries her on his shoulders.

Each night Harry goes to the community hall to meet with the others. He doesn't say anything about these meetings or what's being discussed, but I see the way he shakes his head at Stella when he returns each night. I get no news of Kas. Stella keeps talking about Rose and how we might be able to get her to come and live in the valley, and have the baby here.

Time stretches and, before I know it, a week has passed. Every day I think of Rose. Is she getting better? Are the antibiotics working? Have the Wilders left Angowrie? I toss and turn at night and fret about escaping. But I have to get to Kas first. I can't leave without her.

I've been here for about ten days when I hear Harry and Stella talking quietly after I've gone to bed. I tiptoe into the lounge room and sit on the floor outside their room.

'There's not a chance, Stell. They won't let us,' Harry says. 'It's too dangerous. Ramage's patrols will be out looking for the girl. We could lose everything we've worked for if they track them here.'

'And what about the other girl, Harry? What about Rose?'

'They don't even know if she's real or not. I believe Finn, but Tusker and the others don't. They're not prepared to take the chance, even to get another girl and a baby.'

I can hear the anger in Stella's voice. 'Well, I'm going to help her, Harry. I swear to God, I'm going to. I don't give a damn what the others think.'

'They won't let you leave, Stell. They're watching us like hawks. They'd track you in no time and bring you back.'

'And what about you, Harry?' she says, louder. 'Are you going to lie down and let them trample all over us?'

'You know it's not as easy as that. We've got Willow to consider. If I took off to look for the girl, you two wouldn't be safe. You know what Tusker's like.'

'All right,' Stella says. She leaves a long silence than adds, 'Help Finn and Kas, then. Help them escape.'

Harry is silent. Finally he says, 'You know we'd lose them all. The three of them. They'd never come back to the valley.'

'Four. There'd be four of them, God willing.'

I hear the lamp being blown out in the room and the house falls into darkness. I sit for a while, trying to understand everything I've heard. By the time I get to my feet my knees are cramping and I have to navigate carefully back to my room so I don't knock anything over.

I'm just about to close my door when Stella calls out.

'Goodnight, Finn.'

13

The next afternoon, the decision is taken out of all our hands.

We've just finished lunch when we hear a gunshot. And—with my heart rising into my mouth—the low throttle of a trailbike. Harry reaches behind the dresser and pulls out a double-barrelled shotgun. He lays it on the kitchen table, along with a small bag.

'Stell,' he says. 'It's loaded and there are more cartridges in the bag.'

Seeing me standing in the doorway, he starts talking fast.

'Finn, get Kas. Rachel's place is the one closest to the woolshed with the lemon tree in front. Get her out of here. Head straight up the ridge, as high as you can. Keep climbing until you hit the old logging track. Turn right and eventually you'll get to Pinchgut Junction.'

He moves quickly toward the front door then but stops short of it.

'Good luck, son,' he says.

Then he opens the door and steps outside.

The rumbling of the trailbike comes closer. I look out through a crack in the curtains and see a dozen Wilders standing in the yard. They're armed with an assortment of weapons, from chains to hoes and large knives.

I recognise Ramage immediately, straddling the trailbike, a rifle cradled in his arms. There is a bandage around his hand, and his face is bruised and swollen. There's bright tape around the fuel lines on the trailbike where I cut them. I curse myself for not having thought to slash the tyres too.

Ramage kills the motor and the whole valley is plunged into silence. The men of the community have gathered in front of the house, most of them unarmed.

Ramage grins. 'Well, well, well,' he says. 'Ain't you been the sly ones, tucked away in your little valley here? Selfish bastards keeping this to yourselves.'

He sniffs the wind and makes a show of looking around the buildings.

'Who's in charge here?'

Tusker moves forwards, but Harry holds him by the arm and calls out, 'I am.'

'And who might you be?' Ramage sneers.

'Name's Harry.'

'Harry. You hear that boys? Harry's in charge here. Well, Harry, my name's Benny Ramage and I'm pretty much in charge in this part of the country.'

'Not in this valley, you're not.' Harry's voice is defiant.

I hear movement behind me and I turn to see Stella sitting Willow on the table and picking up the shotgun. She puts her finger to her lips and softly clicks the breach into position. She signals for me to look after Willow, then she slips out the back door with the gun.

'You've got fuck-all chance against us, Harry, and you know it,' Ramage continues. 'You're not fighters, you're farmers. And Christ knows we need farmers, so we don't want to hurt you.'

Ramage lets the silence sit for a minute until he says, 'We could leave you in peace here. But you've got something we want. A boy and a girl. She's a Siley and she belongs to me. We been trackin' them from the coast. The boy tried to kill me last week.'

Again, he leaves the words to hang in the air. I need Harry to stall him. I have to find Kas, but I've got Willow to look after now, too. She has walked across the room and is standing on her tiptoes to see out the window.

'What's happening, Finn?' she whispers. 'Why is Daddy talking to those men?'

'We're all just playing a big game,' I say. 'We're going to hide and the others will try to find us.'

'Where's Mummy?'

'Mummy's hiding,' I say, thinking as quick as I can, 'and we have to sneak out the back as quiet as mice to find her.'

I take her by the hand and move towards the back door. There's a loaf of bread on the dresser that I break in half, shoving a piece into each pocket. It's cold outside. The house backs onto a small holding yard for cattle. It gives us some cover as we move past the side of the house and turn towards the first in the row of sheds. It's awkward running with Willow so I pick her up and piggyback her. She holds on tight around my neck.

When we reach the safety of the woolshed I look back to the men in front of the house. They're still talking.

I pick up movement off to their right. Stella is crouched behind the rusted wreck of a tractor. She has the stock of the shotgun resting against her shoulder and the barrel on the metal seat. She sees us and waves us to keep going.

I run along the back of the shed, but as I turn the corner a hand reaches out from one of the chutes and pulls me down. Willow gives out a little yelp as we stumble and fall sideways. I feel the full force of a body land on top of us and a hand clamps over my mouth.

'It's me.'

'Kas!'

'What's going *on* over there?'

'Ramage,' I say.

I barely get the words out when a blast from a shotgun echoes across the valley, so close I know it must be Stella. There's shouting, then and the sound of a fight, metal on metal, and another blast from the shotgun.

'Come on.' Kas says. 'This is our chance.'

'But he's got a trailbike.'

'I've got something better than that,' she says.

She drags me up by the hand and I pull Willow along behind me. The sheep yards are like a maze. We dodge our way through them and out into the home paddock. Kas leads us along a fence to the back of another shed. She pulls a sheet of corrugated iron aside and squeezes through. I pass Willow in to her, then follow. There's a stall off to the side where a horse stands snorting steam in the cold air. He's jumpy with all the noise, but Kas soothes him. She slips a bridle on and passes the reins over his head.

'Whoa there, Yogi,' she says.

She takes Willow by the hand and opens the stall, while I climb onto the bales and look outside. The fight is still raging in front of Harry's place. I can see a couple of bodies on the ground. There's no sign of Stella behind the tractor and Ramage's trailbike lies on its side in the mud. We've got no chance of getting out of the shed without being seen.

Kas has mounted the horse and has Willow in front of her. She's showing her how to grip the mane. I climb back down and swing my leg over to sit behind Kas.

'Trust me, Finn,' she says. 'Whatever I say, just do it.'

'They'll see us! They have to.'

'Which way do we go? What's the safest way?'

I remember Harry's advice.

'We head up towards the ridge and climb as far as we can.

If we get to the tree line before Ramage, the trailbike won't be able to follow.'

Kas swings around, trying to understand what I'm saying. Then she leans forward and says, 'You hear that, Yogi Bear. He says we gotta make it to the trees. Hold on tight, Willow.'

Then she turns to me. 'Ready?'

Before I get the chance to answer, she digs her heels into Yogi's flanks. He skitters sideways then bursts out into the daylight.

The fight is going on about twenty metres away and everyone seems to stop when they see us. Harry is still standing, and so is Tusker. We're not quite at full gallop when we pass them.

Ramage is the first to react. He moves towards the trailbike. I hear the motor cough a couple of times before it takes. But the noise dies again and I see Harry dragging Ramage from the bike. Kas is leaning forwards, one arm around Willow and the other gripping the reins. We are at full gallop now and heading straight for a railing fence leading to the river paddock.

'Move with me,' Kas yells. 'And hang on!'

Yogi barely misses a step, launching us into the air. I lift off his back altogether but manage to hold onto Kas, who is leaning so far forward she must be squashing Willow. When we land I come down hard and I begin to slip off. Kas reaches around and drags me back into balance.

The paddock is rising steeply towards the trees and she urges Yogi on.

There's still no movement from the houses. I keep expecting to hear the roar of the trailbike. Yogi slows, feeling the incline and the weight of our three bodies, but Kas digs her heels in again and we're in the trees.

The undergrowth is patchy, allowing us to move through at a good pace, but before long the mimosa and bracken fern thicken and we have to slow to a walk. Yogi suddenly seems big and cumbersome in the forest. His flanks are lathered in sweat.

Kas slides off his back and I follow. Willow still hasn't said anything, and I wonder if she saw Harry in the fight.

We try to get a view back to the houses, but since we're only fifty metres into the trees we'll have to keep moving. Above the sound of the wind in the canopy I hear the distinctive revving of the trailbike. Back down in the paddock I spot Ramage riding along the tree line. He revs the bike then veers downhill towards the farmhouses. Through the trees I can just make out a lone figure running up the hill towards us.

It's Stella.

She must have seen us riding off with Willow and has tried to follow. But Ramage has other ideas. He reaches her easily and circles her, his back wheel spitting up a cloud of dust and dirt. Stella keeps edging forwards, but Ramage is tightening the circle. He swoops in and tries to kick her, but Stella jumps out of the way.

While Kas and I have been watching the confrontation below, Willow has slid down off Yogi's back. She starts running in the direction of the paddock, calling to her mother.

I take off after her, but Kas yells, 'Leave her! There's nothing we can do. We've got to take our chance now.'

I'm torn. With just the two of us on Yogi we could move

quickly, maybe make it to Pinchgut Junction before any of Ramage's men and be back in Angowrie by tomorrow. But then I think of Harry and Stella, and how they protected me. And Willow's just a kid caught up in shit she doesn't understand.

Kas leads Yogi further uphill. I can't move; my eyes are fixed on the paddock. Ramage lands a kick to Stella's back and she stumbles. She's quick to her feet, though, and presses on up the hill, forcing Ramage into a wider circle.

Willow has broken cover and is running down towards her mother.

'Sorry,' I say. 'I can't leave them to fight on their own.'

Kas looks at me, then back at the paddock. Without a word, she turns Yogi around and in one movement she's on his back.

'Keep climbing,' she says to me, before digging her heels into Yogi, urging him down the slope.

Somehow she gets him to a canter, then a gallop, as she hugs his back and swings him left and right through the scrub, pulling the reins one way then the other, shifting her weight as Yogi responds to her.

In no time she's out of the trees and making straight for Stella, who has picked up Willow and is trying to protect her from Ramage. I'm not even sure if he sees Kas coming, there is so much dust in the air. Kas has Yogi at full stretch now and I worry she'll run right over the top of Stella and Willow.

But as she nears them, she slows Yogi, putting herself between Stella and Ramage, protecting them with the horse's bulk. Stella reacts fast, passing Willow up to Kas before climbing on herself.

I expect Kas to ride uphill towards me, but she circles back down towards Ramage, who has stopped and is straddling the trailbike with his feet on the ground. As they bear down on the bike, Yogi shies at the last second, almost dislodging Stella, but his flank hits Ramage and knocks him off the bike. Even from this distance I can hear Kas yelling at Ramage, who's lying on the ground, his arms protecting his head. Kas has Yogi skittering and pigrooting around him.

Finally she swings back uphill. When they reach the cover of the trees she slows and slides off to drag Yogi up by the reins. Back in the paddock, a couple of hundred metres from us, Ramage is on his feet again, leaning over and trying to right the trailbike.

No one says anything when they reach me. The air is filled with Yogi's snorting and the sound of branches breaking underfoot as we press up the hill. When the paddock has dropped out of sight we stop and rest. Willow crawls into her mother's arms and Stella looks across at Kas and me. I can't tell whether it's sweat or tears running down her cheeks.

'Thank you,' she says.

Kas brushes her off. She's looking up to the ridge. I know her one thought is to escape, to get as far away from the valley and Ramage as she can. I'm thinking the same thing, but I don't want to leave Stella and Willow.

'We have to keep moving,' Kas says. 'They won't waste any time in coming after us.'

'Not us. Not Willow and me,' Stella says. 'We can't leave. Everything we have is down in the valley.'

Kas is nodding, but I have to speak up.

'You know what'll happen if they're still there, Ramage and his men?'

'I know,' Stella says. 'But Harry's there, and the others. We can't abandon them.'

There's anger in Kas's voice now. 'Sorry, Stella, I was a prisoner down there. I don't owe them anything.'

'That wasn't my doing, Kas. We tried to protect you and Finn at the meeting. I never agreed with the way Sileys were treated.'

'Stella,' I say, 'Kas and me are going back to the coast. We have to go now while we've got the chance. You and Willow can come with us or you can go back to the valley. It's your decision.'

Stella stands up then and holds Willow close to her chest. She whispers something in her ear. Then she turns to Kas and me.

'Take Willow,' she says. 'Please. I can look after myself, but if they took Wils, if they hurt her...' She leaves the sentence hanging.

'No, Mum! No!' Tears are streaming down Willow's cheeks and she clings to her mother even tighter.

'Please!' Stella's voice comes from somewhere deep inside her. Her whole body shakes.

There are no words now. I make my own decision, prising Willow away. She screams and kicks out, but Stella works with me. In the end I have to carry her over my shoulder. I don't look at Kas; I just start walking towards the ridge. I can hear Stella sobbing and Willow is still kicking me and screaming to be put down, but I keep climbing.

'I love you, Wils.' Stella's voice cracks and when I finally look around she's on her knees.

'Look after her,' she mouths. 'Keep her safe.'

'I will. I promise.'

Stella stands up and straightens herself. She turns back towards the valley and begins to thread her way down through the scrub. She doesn't look back.

14

It takes a while for Willow to finally exhaust herself and become a dead weight over my shoulder. Kas is ahead of us, still leading Yogi by the reins. Without the burden of anyone on his back, he seems to be coping better with the climb.

We continue in silence for an hour or so. The rangy stringy-barks give way to manna gums as we climb higher until the rocky crags of the ridge tower over us. The ground is steeper here and Kas pulls hard on Yogi's reins to drag him up.

'Rest,' she says as we come up beside her. I ease Willow off my shoulders. All the defiance has left her little body, though every now and then she chokes back a sob.

Kas sits down and takes Willow in her arms.

'It's okay,' she says. 'We're going to be okay. We'll get you somewhere safe, away from those bad men, then we'll wait there for your mum and dad. But you've got to be strong for us, you understand?'

The day is wearing on and I know we're going to have a rough night. At least it doesn't look like rain, but the clear sky means the temperature will drop away fast. The rocky outcrops are directly above us now. I can't see a way for us to climb much higher, let alone drag Yogi with us.

Kas sees where I'm looking. 'We won't get up there,' she says. 'Not a chance.'

'I know. I reckon our best bet is to go west. Stay at this level if we can and keep an eye out for anywhere we can climb. We'll rest here for a bit then make our way across. There might be an overhang where we can get some shelter for the night.'

We sit in an exhausted silence. Huddled together, I get the chance to look at Kas closely in the daylight. It's hard not to be drawn to the birthmark on her face. It spreads from her hairline, down across her forehead and cheek on the left side. The rest of her face is darkly tanned and her skin is clear. Her hair is thick and matted, jet black like Rose's. But her body is leaner, her arms all sinew and tendon lacing down to large hands. There are calluses across her palms and fingers. Her clothes are torn, with glimpses of her dark skin peeking through.

I find myself wondering where all her strength comes from.

There seems too little of her to ride the way she does, or to drag Yogi up this hill.

'Come on,' Kas says. 'We've got to go.'

It's harder moving across the hill than climbing it. The ground is flinty underfoot and we struggle to keep from falling. Willow is on Yogi's back, and while the horse keeps slipping he always seems to right himself without Willow falling.

We continue like this for a couple of hours or so. It seems impossible that the day has passed so quickly but the sky is beginning to darken and a chill is finding its way into the undergrowth.

'Kas,' I say. 'I'm going to climb higher up towards the cliffs and walk parallel to you. I'll keep you in sight. If I find shelter, I'll whistle.'

She nods and keeps walking. I begin clambering towards the cliffs. The ground flattens out at the base of the rock so it's easy to keep pace with Kas and Yogi.

It's almost dark by the time I find a small overhang where the ground has been trodden flat, probably by animals looking for shelter. I whistle and I hear Kas begin to urge Yogi up towards me. It takes her a good ten minutes to climb up. I have to lean down and help her drag Yogi the last few metres. Once he's on the flat I take Willow off his back and put her down on the dry ground under the overhang. She pushes back against the wall and hugs her knees to her chest. Kas wanders off to tether Yogi to a tree.

I drop into the bush and collect as much bracken as I can

hold. It won't be much, but it will help to keep the cold at bay.

We can't risk a fire—not with Ramage's men after us. I spread the bracken on the ground and sit down next to Willow. She crawls in closer for warmth. Kas eases herself down further along the wall.

'I'm hungry,' a small voice says against my chest.

'Sorry, Wils,' I say. 'We might be able to catch something tomorrow.'

'What about the bread?' she says.

'What bread?'

'In your pocket.'

With everything that's happened I'd totally forgotten about the bread I grabbed from the dresser before Willow and I escaped out the backdoor.

The bread has crumbled in my pockets, but there is enough for each of us to have a small piece.

'Your mum makes good bread, Wils,' I say without thinking.

Her chin drops to her chest with the mention of her mother and even in the half-dark I can see her bottom lip start to quiver. Kas moves over and puts her arm around her, and we squeeze her between us. Eventually Willow lays her head down in Kas's lap and closes her eyes. Before long we can hear her steady breaths as she sleeps.

'I'm going to have a last look about,' I whisper to Kas, 'before it gets too dark.'

I retrace my steps for about a hundred metres, listening for any movement below us. Apart from a breeze moving through the branches of the trees up on the ridge, the bush is quiet.

Back at the overhang I can just make out Kas and Willow. I sit down next to them.

'Is Rose okay?' Kas asks.

I close my eyes and think of the last time I saw her, propped up in bed, sipping soup. 'She wasn't great when I left her. Had a fever, but I think she was getting over it.'

'And the baby?'

'Okay, I think. It was kicking.'

'That's a good sign.' She shifts her position and I feel her shoulder against mine. 'How far is Angowrie?'

'We can make it in a day if we can get up to the ridge and find the track.'

She takes time to think this over.

'Why did you come looking for me?' she says. 'You were safe down there. Or, at least, safer than anywhere else.'

'Rose would have come on her own if I hadn't tried. I couldn't let her do that. And she says she might be further along than she looks. Six months, maybe.'

'I reckon more. Her boobs are big.' She laughs. 'She's always been flat as a pancake.'

She's quiet again until she says, 'What do you think's happened back in the valley, after we went?'

'Who knows? I only hope Harry and Stella are all right. They were good to me.'

'Maybe Ramage'll be more worried about chasing us than hassling them. It's us he wants.'

I peer out into the dark. 'I'm not sure that's so great. We've got a head start on them, but they know the country better than we do.'

Kas lifts Willow off her lap and eases her between us. Then we lie down and snuggle in as close as we can.

'Thanks,' Kas says.

'For what?'

'For helping Rose.'

As exhausted as I am, sleep is nearly impossible. The wind picks up and pushes harder through the treetops, its gusts filling the overhang with the sounds of the bush. I wake a dozen times throughout the night, each time taking a few seconds to work out where I am. It's freezing. Despite the bracken, the cold still pushes up through the earth underneath us. Willow snuggles in closer, burying her face in my jumper. Kas reaches her arm over and hold us both. I do the same and feel the skin of her shoulder. It's cold and smooth and soft.

15

It's not a great feeling, waking up in the morning cold and hungry. When I open my eyes, Kas's face is only inches away. Her lips are moving, like she's having a conversation in her sleep. Her eyes spring open and there's an awkward moment when we breathe each other's breath. Her eyes are deeper and darker than Rose's—if that's even possible.

We both roll away, leaving Willow to sleep. It's barely light, but the birds are filling the forest with their songs. Kas goes to check on Yogi while I head off in the other direction for a piss.

When I come back Kas laughs.

'You're walking a little bow-legged there, cowboy,' she says.

The insides of my thighs are tender from riding Yogi, even if it was only for a few minutes.

'I think it was the jumping,' I say. 'You nearly lost me there, you know.'

'I'm not used to jumping bareback, but Yogi knew what he was doing. He's had a cold night. He's a tough old bugger, though.'

'We'd better get moving,' I say. 'We've got to find a way up to the top. Get to that old logging track Harry told me about. It'll take us to Pinchgut Junction and from there we can make the coast in a few hours. We could be home by tonight.'

'We're going to need food,' Kas says. 'And water. For us and for Yogi.'

Willow is awake now and standing under the overhang. She looks at us warily. 'Are we going home today, Finn?' she asks.

'Not yet,' I reply. 'But soon, okay?'

By the time we start moving, low cloud has rolled in and blanketed the cliffs above us. But once the sun comes up the bush begins to warm. Steam evaporates off the rock faces and the clouds lift from the cliff tops. The crags aren't as steep here; they taper more gently up to the ridge. Further along, the rocks give way to a gully filled with mountain ash and tree ferns.

The ground is softer too, and I can hear water trickling under the lower ferns. We climb down as best we can, slipping and sliding as we get closer to the water. Finally we reach a break in the ferns where the creek flows between moss-covered banks. The ground is boggy and Yogi's hooves sink under his weight, but he steps out into the stream and stands in the water.

The three of us move upstream of him and lie on our bellies to drink. The water is cold but refreshing. I splash it up on my face and over my hair. Kas has taken her boots off and has her feet dangling in the water. She smiles. The sun filters down through the fern fronds and I find a spot to sit in its warmth. Willow comes and joins me. Her hands ferret in my pockets and pull out the last of the breadcrumbs.

Kas has headed further upstream, where she takes off her jumper, then peels her top up over her head. With her back to me, I can see the knobs of her vertebrae like buttons down the middle of her back as she leans over and splashes her arms and chest with water.

'Nice spot for a picnic,' she says when she's back, dressed again.

'Excellent,' I say, putting on a toffy voice. Willow smiles for the first time this morning.

'I've cut some sandwiches,' Kas says, dropping her hands into an imaginary basket. 'Now, Miss Willow, I have peanut butter, jam or cucumber.'

'What's peanut butter,' she says. 'Butter comes from cows.' Kas and I glance at each other.

'I remember peanut butter,' I say. 'I was a crunchy man, myself.'

'Smooth for me,' Kas says.

Willow looks at us like we're speaking a foreign language. Kas hands her an imaginary sandwich.

'Is this blackberry or raspberry jam?' Willow asks, playing along now.

'Which one do you like best?' Kas asks.

'Blackberry!'

'Then blackberry it is.'

Willow takes a big bite and pretends to chew.

'Scrumptious,' she says, and we all laugh.

But the game falls away quickly. We are going to struggle without food. Kas leads Yogi out of the stream. I figure if we follow the water we might be lucky and find our way to the top.

It's slow going. The mud sucks at our boots and Yogi has to duck under the low-hanging branches and ferns. Eventually the banks give way to rock again, and we are able to climb out onto slabs that aren't too steep.

Kas keeps to the edges with Yogi while Willow and I scout ahead for the best route. We are a good twenty metres above Kas when I look back to see her pulling in vain on Yogi's reins. He has come as far as he can in the steep terrain. He's a lather of sweat again, digging in his front hooves and leaning back against Kas's efforts.

'Stay there, Kas,' I yell. 'Let him rest. I'm going to see how far it is to the top.'

I'm able to move fast, and before long the rock slabs grow wider and the bush thins out on either side. The forest opens out into an old logging coup with a track winding its way up to the very top of the ridge. Over in one corner I can see a pile of logs and a flatbed truck almost completely overgrown by weeds and vines.

When I go back and tell Kas what I've found, her face brightens.

'I don't think Yogi will make it, though,' I say. 'It's really steep and slippery. We might have to let him go, Kas.'

She steps out onto the slab and surveys the incline, then heads off to get Yogi.

'He won't make it,' I call after her. 'He's got no grip on the rocks. You can't lead him up.'

'Watch me,' she says defiantly.

Before I can say anything more, she has swung herself up onto Yogi's back. Straightaway she drops the reins low on either side of his neck, leans forward and reassures him with long, steady pats.

This is mad, I think, especially when we are so close to making it to the top. I can't let her do it.

I reach out to grab the reins, but she checks Yogi and backs away.

'Finn,' she says, calmly. 'Take Willow and show me the best route. I'm going to watch from here.'

'Have I got a choice?' I ask.

'No.'

I take Willow's hand and retrace my steps up the sloping rocks. Every now and again I turn and call to Kas, while at the same time laying fallen branches out on the rock shelf, marking the route.

Finally I lay one across the path where they need to turn into the bush, but it'll be a miracle if they make it this far. It's steeper than I thought.

'Careful,' I yell and I see Kas wave. Willow and I move out onto the rock shelf to watch.

Kas starts to climb, gently urging Yogi up the slab and shifting her weight to keep them both balanced. They start off okay, but halfway up they come to a mossy section and I see Kas hesitate. Her eyes dart back and forth across the rock, searching for the best route. She gives the slightest nudge to Yogi's flanks and he edges forwards. Half-a-dozen times his hooves begin to slip, but she corrects him before he has time to panic.

They're soon within a few steps of the turn into the bush, though they still have a gap of close to a metre to negotiate where a crack splits the rock. Willow and I are just above them now.

I can hear Kas soothing Yogi. 'Last little bit, boy. If we can get over here we're home free. We'll be in the bush and it'll all be over. I promise.'

The sweat is dripping off Yogi and his muscles quiver. Now that she's closer, I can see that Kas is sweating too. She wipes her hands on her pants and steadies herself again.

In one quick movement she lunges, taking Yogi with her. She tries to turn him into the bush, but he barely gets his front legs up before he starts to slip. His back legs splay as he slides slowly towards the drop. In one movement, Kas throws herself forwards, lifting the reins over Yogi's head and landing on the rock above him. She holds the reins tight and braces herself. Yogi's eyes are wide with terror.

Quietly, without any hint of panic in her voice, Kas says, 'Finn, move towards me. Slow. Don't spook him or he's gone.'

I edge down the rock until I'm beside her.

'Now,' she whispers, 'take the reins and keep them taut.

When I say, pull with everything you've got.'

She starts to inch her way along Yogi's flank, stroking him all the way down to his back legs. She makes a soothing ticking noise with her tongue.

'You ready, Finn?' she says. 'Don't pull suddenly, just increase the pressure.'

'Now?' I say.

'*Now.*'

Kas has disappeared from view behind Yogi. I begin to pull, feeling his whole weight against me. I hear his hooves skitter, but I soon realise Kas is under him at the back, placing herself between him and the drop and pushing his legs. I don't know how it happens but Yogi finds some grip and lunges past me, hitting me flush in the chest and knocking me to the side. He crashes into the undergrowth.

I look back to see Kas lying flat on the rock on her stomach. My blood runs cold—until she props herself up and smiles.

'See,' she says. 'Easy!'

Willow climbs down off the rock above us and throws herself at Kas, who catches her. Then the two of them edge across to sit down next to me in the fringes of the bush. Kas is limping heavily.

'You okay?' I ask.

'Just a kick to the thigh. It's not the first—and it won't be the last. You?'

'Fine. Just winded.'

'Come on,' she says struggling to her feet. 'Let's find Yogi.'

It's easy to follow his tracks through the bush. He's forced his way through to the logging coup and found some grass on the edge of the old track. His flanks are scratched and bloody and there's a cut halfway up his front leg, but otherwise he looks okay.

We collapse into the grass. Kas flexes her leg, trying to keep the muscles moving, while Willow dozes in the sun. I know we have to get moving to have any chance of getting back to Angowrie by nightfall, but there's such a sense of relief that we've found our way up the ridge that I just want to enjoy it for a moment.

Kas winces as she gets to her feet. She's in more pain than she's letting on.

'Show me,' I say.

She turns her back, undoes her belt and eases her jeans down to her knees. I hear her intake of breath when she sees it for the first time.

'How does it look?' I say, still sitting down.

'Like I've been kicked by a fucking horse,' she says.

She turns around. There is an almost perfect half-moon welt in the middle of her thigh.

'There goes your modelling career,' I say, keeping the smile from my face.

'Yeah, I was thinking the same thing,' she says. 'But I reckon this'd already done that,' she says pointing to her birthmark. 'Not much work for freaks.'

She turns her back to me again and pulls her jeans up.

'It's okay,' she says, trying to smile. 'I'm used to it. Mostly I forget it's there, until I hear the whispers and see the sideways glances.'

She fusses with her belt, straightens her T-shirt and pushes the hair off her face.

'Rose tell you about Longley? The feedstore?' she asks, still looking away.

'A bit. Enough.'

'It's the only time being a freak was any advantage. The men stayed away from me.'

'You're not a freak. You're...beautiful.'

The words slip out before I can stop them.

She laughs, but it's bitter. 'I don't need your sympathy, Finn,' she says. She pauses. 'Horses, they like me. They don't care how I look.'

Willow has woken up.

'Can I ride on Yogi, Kas?' she asks.

'Sure you can,' Kas says and moves over to pick her up. But when she bends down her leg buckles underneath her and she falls.

'I think there might be two of you riding Yogi,' I say.

'I can walk,' Kas snaps.

'Not if we want to get to Angowrie today.'

She doesn't respond, but continues to flex her leg.

'I'm going to look around the old truck for something we can carry water in,' I say.

I have to fight my way through creepers and undergrowth to get to the truck. The doors are rusted closed, but I manage to prise one open. There's a plastic water bottle wedged under the seat.

I head back through the bush to fill it in the creek. I have to crawl out onto the rock slab and lie on my belly to get the bottle under the flowing water. As I'm crouched over the creek, I hear another noise. Men's voices.

I keep low until I'm back in the cover of the bush, then I take off as fast as I can.

Kas struggles to her feet when she sees me running towards her. I don't need to tell her. She lifts Willow onto Yogi's back, but struggles to climb up herself. I get to her side and boost her up.

'How many?' she asks.

'Dunno. But we've gotta move. Now!'

16

I'm not sure if Yogi senses the danger, but he seems suddenly more lively. He breaks into a trot, heading up the track along the side of the coup. I have one arm around Kas's waist and she holds Willow in front of her.

Kas's talking to Yogi. 'Come on, boy,' she says. 'Just give us ten minutes. We need to get a break on them.'

I keep looking back to the spot where we came out of the bush at the bottom of the coup, but there's no sign of movement. The track we are on re-enters the forest closer to the top, concealing us from anyone further down.

Eventually, Kas slips off Yogi's back and I follow. Willow

stays on to ride for a while.

'So, did you see them?' Kas asks.

'No. But I heard them.'

The track widens as we get closer to the ridgeline, where we come to a T-intersection.

'I reckon this is the logging track that meets the coast road just below Pinchgut Junction,' I say. 'If Ramage's men are still guarding the cutting, we should be able to avoid them.'

'How far do you reckon?' Kas asks.

'Hard to tell, but it can't be more than ten ks.'

As we move along the track I keep my eye out for prickly currant bushes. They're about the only bush food I know. There's plenty of them in the scrub down closer to Angowrie. The bright red berries are easy to spot. I tell Kas, and she starts looking off into the bush as well.

It takes us a couple of hours to get to the coast road. We don't hesitate, swinging south as the road starts to descend. It's mid-afternoon by then and my energy is draining away. Kas is limping badly now, but she refuses to ride.

'And I thought your sister was stubborn,' I mutter.

She lets that go but, with her back to me, says, 'I reckon you fell for Rose. Makes sense. A boy on his own for years, then a beautiful girl is chased into town. I bet if she had been a boy you wouldn't have been so quick to help.'

When she turns back I can see she's smiling.

'If she was a boy,' I say, 'Ramage wouldn't have been chasing her.'

The sun is still high enough to warm us when the road swings briefly out of the shadows. I can hear kookaburras in the distance and every now and again the snapping of twigs as a wallaby takes off into the undergrowth. At one point I think I pick up the smell of the ocean.

Kas is ahead of me. She's taken her jumper off and the dark skin on her arms glints with sweat.

'There is something I've been wondering,' I say, 'but I don't know how to put it...'

'What?'

'You know, Rose being pregnant...'

'Do I know who the father is?' She shrugs. I'm not sure if it's an I-don't-care shrug or an I-don't-know one.

'Finn, look!' she shouts, leading Yogi off the road. She's found a currant bush.

'Careful,' I say, 'the leaves are really prickly.'

There's not a lot of fruit, but I show her how to shake the branches at their base to make the berries fall.

Willow climbs down off Yogi and picks up the berries. They are sweet and juicy, little grenades of flavour on our tongues. Conversation drops away as we gorge ourselves.

Kas has trickles of red at the sides of her mouth. She grins and her teeth are all stained.

'They're so good. What do you reckon, Willow?' she asks.

'Nice,' she agrees, smearing the red juice down the side of her face. 'Look,' she says. 'I'm like you, Kas.'

It's not until I get my first glimpse of the ocean, that blue horizon I have been missing for the last week, that I dare to think we might make it home safely. I'm so worried about Rose—whether she'll still be there, whether she's managed to stay safe, whether she will be well enough to recognise us.

I keep an eye out for the windmill and tank on my left, though the fading light doesn't help. Eventually it appears out of the gloom. And my bike is still there.

'Aren't you full of surprises!' Kas says when I wheel it out.

The sun drops below the horizon and the night sets in. I don't know what to expect when we get back into Angowrie, but I have to assume Ramage has left someone there to keep watch.

By now Kas can hardly move her leg and I've finally convinced her to ride up with Willow. I wheel the bike beside them. We must look like a strange trio.

I decide it's best to get off the road, so we turn down the track towards the hayshed. The collapsed iron roof and steel frame are all that's left of it. The wire I strung across the gate to knock Ramage from his bike is coiled by one of the fence posts. It still makes me shudder to think about cutting him with the knife.

The familiar feeling of coming home has crept up on me. The only difference now is that I'm bringing two people—and there's another one waiting for me. And I've almost forgotten about Rowdy. I can't wait to give him a scratch behind the ears and to have him dance around my feet again. But I have to keep a lid on my excitement. I don't want to get lazy and stuff up now. I have to stay alert, even though I'm completely buggered.

I take Willow off Yogi's back first and help Kas down next. I'm beginning to think her injury may be more serious than a bruise. It's dark by now, but I can hear her sharp intake of breath when she walks.

I ride ahead on my bike to check things out, finding myself at the top of our street in a couple of minutes. I can see all the way down the hill to the Wilders' camp on the river. There's no sign of movement, no fire, and I can't smell smoke.

I stay close to the fences until I'm within a hundred metres of my place, then I move in for cover, crossing through the yards of the deserted houses.

I stop at our fence, lean the bike against a tree and check the house. Inching along the side of the shed, I give Rose the warning whistle and wait.

When I come in closer I see the back door is wide open. I whistle again.

'Rose,' I whisper as loud as I dare.

When the wind drops for a few seconds I hear a faint whining coming from the kitchen. Stepping through the door my heart jumps into my mouth. Even in the darkness I can tell the place is a mess: the table is turned over, chairs are broken and most of the drawers have been pulled out and emptied onto the floor. The whining sound turns to laboured breathing, heavy and nasally. It's Rowdy.

When my eyes adjust to the gloom, I find him lying in the hallway, his body pushed against the wall. He tries to get up, but his back legs give way under him.

'Rose,' I call again, louder this time. There's no response.

I scoop up Rowdy, carry him out onto the back porch and check him over. He's been in a fight. I can't see any wounds, but there are lumps where he has been hit or kicked. He looks so thin; he can't have eaten in a week. His tongue lolls out the side of his mouth. I leave him there and get a bowl of water. He raises his head just enough to drink from it.

'What's happened, boy,' I ask. 'Where's Rose?'

I lay him down again and go back into the house, checking each room. Everywhere else looks untouched; it's just the kitchen that's a mess. The bed where I left Rose is unmade, but the room doesn't smell of her. I don't think she's been here for a while.

Rowdy is a little more lively when I get back out to the porch. He lifts his head and tries to wag his tail.

'I'll be back as soon as I can,' I tell him.

He whines when I disappear into the dark again. It tears me up to leave him like this, even for a short time, but I have to bring Kas and Willow in. They'll be worried that something has happened to me.

Spooked by what I've seen at the house, I'm extra cautious and leave the bike. I find Willow and Kas lying in the grass together. Willow is asleep with her head in Kas's lap. I can hear Yogi grazing not far away.

'Where's Rose?' Kas asks. 'Is she safe?'

'She's not there. It doesn't look good. The place is a mess and Rowdy, my dog, he's been injured.'

Kas sags. 'She might be okay though mightn't she, Finn?' she says. 'She might have run?'

'It's possible. Lets go down to the house,' I say. 'I know it's dangerous, but we need shelter and food tonight. And I have to look after Rowdy.'

Rowdy's still lying where I left him. When he hears me again, he struggles to his feet and hobbles to the edge of the porch.

Kas has tethered Yogi in the backyard. At the backdoor, she approaches Rowdy with her hand out saying, 'Hello, Rowdy. Hello, boy.'

She scratches him gently under the muzzle, then behind his ears.

'Let's get inside,' I say.

Kas picks up Rowdy and carries him into the house.

'Is there food here, Finn?' asks Willow, following behind her.

'Yep, as long as it hasn't been stolen.'

Inside, Kas and I stand the table up and find two chairs that aren't broken. I notice one of the drawers under the sink hasn't been disturbed, the one that had the torch in it. Sure enough, it's still there. And working.

Kas and Willow are startled by the sudden light.

'Bloody hell, Finn, a torch! I haven't seen one of those for ages. You've got batteries?' Kas asks.

'Not many left now, but, yeah, I've got a few.'

'What's happened here?'

'Dunno. I'm guessing the Wilders found the place, but there's no way of knowing if Rose was here when they did.'

While Kas starts to clean up, I go out to check the food supplies. The branch across the door is still in place and the padlock too. I grab a few tins of baked beans. Then, while Kas and Willow look on in amazement, I cook the beans and serve them up on plates. I offer Rowdy some, spooning them into his mouth. He eats a little but then backs away. Kas has been checking him out, running her hand over his coat. One of his back legs is swollen below the hip and is sensitive to her touch.

'You and me, Rowdy,' she says. 'Cripples, the both of us.'

We eat in the dark. I don't want to waste batteries after I've finished cooking. There's plenty of slurping and scraping of plates. When we've finished, I carry Willow up to Rose's room and put her to bed. It still smells of spew.

Back in the kitchen, I can just make out Kas's silhouette against the white of the wall behind her.

'What now?' she asks.

'We'll have a look around in the morning, try to work out what's happened.'

'What if she got away? Where would she go?'

'Ray's. But she'd have to...' I jump to my feet and switch the torch on.

'The map,' I say. 'I hid the map and told her where to find it. In the flour tin.'

I reach under the sink, pull off the lid and shine the torch inside.

'It's empty! She's taken the map. She's tried to get to Ray's place.'

'Who's Ray?'

I explain quickly.

'What if the Wilders have caught her? What if they've got the map now?'

'We'll find out soon enough. I'll go out to Ray's tomorrow and see if everything is okay.'

'No, you won't.' Her voice cuts through the dark.

'What?'

'No way are you going to leave Willow and me here. We're coming too. This place isn't safe if the Wilders know about it.'

'You're injured, Kas. You won't make it.'

'Watch me,' she says.

I fold my arms. 'We'll talk about it tomorrow.'

'You can talk about it all you like, but Willow and me are coming with you.'

I'm too tired to argue.

'You can sleep in with Willow,' I say. 'I'll be in the front room.'

I lead Rowdy to the bedroom. I've hardly got the strength to lift him onto the bed. I lie down next to him and put my hand on his belly, feeling him breathe in and out.

Before I doze off, I try to think how long it's been since I did this, lie here with Rowdy next to me, listening to him breathing. Before Rose, before the Wilders, before Kas and Willow. It can't be more than a couple of weeks, but it feels like a lifetime.

17

In the morning I wake to the sound of sweeping and drawers being replaced. It takes me a minute to work out where I am and what's happened in the last twenty-four hours.

Kas has just about got the kitchen back to its usual state. She's wearing a long T-shirt I recognise. It was one of Dad's. Her legs are bare.

'Hope you don't mind,' she says. 'I just couldn't sleep in my clothes. They're so grotty. I stole some of your mum's undies, too.'

'No worries. Someone might as well wear them.'

'I didn't mean to wake you. I was up early and thought I might...'

'You're like your sister.'

'Ha, she'd laugh at that. She was always banging on about me riding horses instead of doing my share of the chores.'

'How's Willow?'

'Still asleep, poor thing.'

I yawn and stretch. 'How'd you sleep?'

'On and off. You?'

'Same. How's the leg?'

'Stiff. I've had worse kicks before, though.'

She lifts the shirt. The bruise on her thigh is a deep purple and it looks larger than it did yesterday.

'It looks worse than it feels,' she says. 'I've always been a bruiser.'

We are standing with the table between us. She drops the shirt and looks around the kitchen.

'You been outside yet?' I ask.

'Had a quick look. No sign of anyone. Just Yogi eating up the backyard. I checked him over. He'll be okay, I reckon.'

'Bunch of invalids you lot. Rowdy, Yogi, you. Only seven good legs between you.'

She laughs, short and sharp, then sits down at the table.

'So, what's for breakfast?' she asks.

I grin. 'Come with me.'

I take her next door where I pull back the branch and unlock the door. Her reaction is the same as Rose's had been: she hobbles between the shelves, touching everything, running her hands over the labels, stopping to read them aloud.

'Heinz canned tomatoes. Edgell green peas, Home Brand sausages and gravy.'

'Not my favourite,' I say, 'but Rowdy loves them.'

I grab some more beans and a sausages and gravy and usher her out the door. I give her the tins and ask her to go back inside and heat them up while I hunt for something else.

'What?' she says. 'What are you hiding?'

'Wait and see,' I call over my shoulder, heading around behind the shed. The nest in the low cypress tree three doors down is full of eggs. I make a basket out of the front of my jumper and carry them to the house.

'Omelettes for brekkie, anyone?' I call when I'm back in the kitchen. Willow is sitting up at the table and claps her hands. Kas just shakes her head and laughs.

It's the best breakfast I've ever eaten. There are enough eggs to make half-a-dozen omelettes, and with the beans heated and spread over the top it's a feast. Even Rowdy gets excited, limping out to the kitchen and resting his muzzle in Kas's lap. I open the can of sausages and he wolfs them down, licking the bowl for a few minutes just to make sure he's got everything.

'It's a good sign he's eating,' says Kas.

Eventually Rowdy retreats to his blanket in the corner and eases himself down. He's still in pain.

Willow has also cleaned up her plate, licking it for good measure. Kas laughs and does the same.

'Soooooo good,' she murmurs.

When we're all done, we push our plates away and sit back,

enjoying the feeling of a full stomach. But we can't relax for long. We have to decide on our next move.

'How far is Ray's?' Kas asks.

'It will take us a couple of hours. We'll have to get Yogi out to Ray's, anyway—we can't hide him in town. I think I should go and scout around first. Chances are Ramage's men have tracked us. We'll have to be careful. We don't want to lead them to Ray's. My guess is they'll have camped up near the hayshed. It'll be safer to travel after dark so we can rest up until then. Sound like a plan?'

'Sounds like a plan,' Kas says.

'Finn.' Willow finally speaks up. 'When will Mummy and Daddy be coming?'

Kas exchanges a glance with me and puts her arm around Willow. 'Soon,' she says. 'You've got to be brave until they get here. Can you do that?'

'How long for?'

'I don't know, sweetie. But I'm sure they're going to come as soon as they can.'

Kas pulls Willow closer.

'They'll be okay, Wils. Don't worry.'

I spend the morning checking around town, jumping fences and slipping through gates to get down near the river. The rest of town looks just like it has for the last two years, with the shops burnt out, the petrol station with its big yellow Shell sign and grass eating its way up through cracks in the roads.

My last stop is the platform above the river mouth. I need

to see the ocean again. The wind is onshore and the waves small, but the big stretch of beach pulls at me like a magnet.

I make my way along the top of the dunes for about a hundred metres, double-checking that it's clear, then I wind my way down to the beach. In the last of tea tree before the sand, I strip off my clothes and boots and run full pelt into the water.

It's so cold I'm sure my balls are up around my ears, but it's also the best feeling. I can taste the salt in my mouth and feel the water rushing over me.

I stand up in waist-deep water on the sandbar and dive under the waves as they jack up and throw themselves at me. Then I swim out further, to the unbroken waves. I turn and kick with the first one and feel myself being lifted and thrown towards the beach. It's like wrestling with an old friend, tumbling underneath then coming up for air.

I enjoy the walk back in familiar surroundings, knowing the sounds of it, the lie of the land. I know I can outsmart anyone coming into my territory, trick them into thinking I'm going one way, then double back to watch them get confused. It's only a small town, but it's big enough to hide in.

As I cross Parker Street something catches my eye, something out of place. Over in the corner of a vacant block there's a lump on the ground. It looks like a body.

I slip through the gate in the paling fence, which gives me enough cover to get close. I don't want to think about the possibility of it being Rose.

I peek over the top of the fence. It's a man, lying on his

back. His hair and beard are matted with dirt and leaves. In the middle of his chest is a knife buried to its handle.

I climb to the top of the fence, drop into the vacant lot and crawl over to the body. I say body, because I'm pretty sure he's been dead for a while. His face is white behind his beard and when I touch his arm it's stiff and cold. I don't recognise him, but then, with their long hair and beards, the Wilders all look alike.

Something strikes me as familiar, though. The knife. It's out of my kitchen. The familiar adrenaline courses through me.

I turn away, take the knife by the handle and draw it out of his chest. There is a squeaking, gurgling sound that I never want to hear again. I can't look at his face with its blank stare any longer, so I heave him over onto his side, then onto his stomach. It's only when he settles in the grass again that I see the arrow, its shaft broken off, its head lodged in the back of his thigh. It's one of my arrows.

My heart gives a leap as I realise it must have been Rose who shot him. I don't want to think of her stabbing him in the chest, but I conjure up the image of her chasing him and shooting the arrow into his leg, bringing him down.

It doesn't seem decent to leave him here in the paddock, but I've got no choice. It only takes me a couple of minutes to reach the backyard, where I give a whistle.

Kas appears on the porch and waves me in. I decide not to tell her about the man.

'You hair's wet,' she says as soon as I step into the kitchen.

'I went for a quick swim.'

'In the ocean?'

'Yeah.'

'Is it safe?'

'Why?'

'Why'd you reckon? We could do with a wash too, couldn't we Wils,' she says.

'You can wash here. We've got water; the sea's freezing.'

'The sun's coming out. It'll be warmer this afternoon.'

'We can't take the risk. We've made it this far; we don't want to blow it now.'

'What? So it's okay for you to have a swim, but not us? Is that what you're saying? What if we just decide to go, anyway?'

'You don't know the beach. You don't know where it's safe to swim.'

'But...' She hesitates and looks around the room.

'What?'

'It's gonna sound stupid.'

'Try me.'

'I've never been to the beach.'

I can hardly believe what she's saying.

'You mean, never?'

She shakes her head.

'How's that possible. Didn't you ever go on holidays?'

'I'm a Siley, remember. The furthest we ever went with Stan and Beth was into Longley. That was it.'

'What about before you were sent to the farm?'

'I only remember bits of the boat trip. We were kept below decks. It stank of diesel and I was sick the whole time.'

It's a stupid risk to take, but I do want to show them the beach, especially since Kas's never seen one.

'Maybe we could walk out to the point,' I say. 'There are some rock pools tucked around the corner that you can't see from the main beach. I could take my snorkelling gear and maybe grab some abalone or even a cray. We could take them out to Ray. He'd love that.'

A smile spreads across Kas's face.

'But first we'll have to get ourselves organised for tonight,' I say.

We spend the rest of the morning preparing to leave. I tie two hessian sacks together to make saddlebags we can throw over Yogi, while Kas goes through Mum's clothes and stuffs a selection into my old schoolbag.

While she's in the bedroom with Willow, I clean the knife I found in the Wilder's chest and put it back in the drawer. It's going to be hard to use it again without thinking of where it's been.

Rowdy has been getting more active, following me around the house since I got back from the beach. I'm starting to think he had been hungry more than anything. He hasn't lost the limp, but he seems to be getting some of his strength back. Still, I'm not going to risk taking him with us to the beach. He needs to rest up for tonight.

Lunch is beans again and two new eggs I find in the nest. Hopefully we'll have fish for dinner. Outside, the sun is now high and the wind has eased off.

Rowdy isn't happy about being left behind in the house so I leave some scraps in his bowl to keep him busy. Kas has pulled on an old skirt of Mum's and limps along behind me with the bag of clean clothes. Willow sticks close by.

I avoid the paddock with the body by taking a detour and coming out higher on Parker Street. There's a track that follows the cliff tops. We could walk around the beach to the point, but that'd leave us too exposed. Up here we're still in the cover of the tea tree and low stringybarks.

'Finn!'

Kas has stopped at a gap in the trees and is looking out at the ocean.

'It's beautiful!'

She has her arms outstretched and the wind coming off the sea blows her hair off her face.

'You didn't tell me it was so big! And the colour... It's like nothing I've ever seen before.'

I can't help smiling. 'It's a bit chopped up today. You should see it when the offshore's blowing and the sets are lining up.'

She looks at me, bewildered. 'I have no idea what you're talking about, but it sounds amazing.'

'I'll explain later,' I say, taking her arm and pulling her along. 'We don't have time now.'

The rock pools are like big potholes in the reef when it's exposed at low tide, deep and perfectly clear. We walk out to the rock shelf. Kas keeps stopping to pick up shells, kelp and cuttlefish. She runs her finger around the rim of an abalone shell.

I show her and Willow the safest pool to swim in, then I

strip off to my shorts, take my snorkel, mask and catch bag, and drop off the ledge into deep water. It's colder out here than back in the bay and straightaway I regret not bringing my wetsuit. The swell is bigger than I would like too, but it's not breaking over the reef.

I wait on the surface to get my breath, then dive. There is a blue down here different from up on the surface—it presses in on you and darkens as you go deeper. The sun filters down in shafts but eventually they're swallowed by the blue too.

I know exactly where I'll find abalone. I unsheathe the knife and dive down a couple of metres. Dad showed me years ago how to slide the knife in under them and twist it to lever them off the rock. I have to come back up a few times for air, but before too long I've got eight good-sized ones.

I surface and start to climb out of the water.

'Stay there,' Kas shouts when I clamber back up onto the reef. 'Willow and me aren't ready yet.'

Their heads and shoulders are poking out of the rock pool.

'Turn around,' Kas calls. 'We have to get dressed.'

I sit on the edge of the shelf and look back along the coast to where Red Rock juts out in the distance. If Rose followed the map she would have travelled that way to Ray's. Tonight can't come fast enough—we need to get out there and make sure she's safe. I sneak a quick look to see if they're ready. Kas, who is leaning over to help Willow out of the water, just has a singlet and a pair of undies on. They stick to her wet skin and the sun catches on the water dripping from her hair onto her back and legs. As she lowers Willow down on the rocks, she sees me staring.

'You perving, Finn?' she says. I can hear a snigger in her voice. I look away.

Next thing I know she's squatting down beside me, close enough for her hair to be touching my shoulder.

'The water's so salty!' she says. 'But it feels amazing. I love it.'

She puts her hand on my arm. Her skin is cold enough to spread goosebumps along my wrist.

'What you got?' she asks.

I try to act natural, even though all I can think about is her body next me, dripping wet, and her breasts pushing against her singlet.

'Um...a heap of abs.'

I open the bag for her. Kas calls Willow over to have a look.

'Come on,' I say. 'We'd better head back.'

The sun is getting low and the wind has dropped away. Kas walks in front while I piggyback Willow, who's too tired now not to accept a ride.

'Stop looking at my bum,' Kas says without turning around.

Willow giggles. I wonder how Kas even knew.

We make it home just as the sky is starting to darken. We creep along, but there's no sign of movement in the yard except for Yogi's big silhouette. He lifts his head to check us out then goes back to munching the grass.

Rowdy is waiting by the door to greet us. Willow pats him, and he follows her into the lounge room. The house is quiet, just Kas and me tiptoeing around each other, and the sound of Willow talking to Rowdy. The room seems small all of a sudden and I'm aware of Kas in the space, the way she moves, the way her hair falls over her face when she leans forwards. It's like we're doing some sort of weird dance, trying to avoid each other but not really wanting to. I empty the abs into the sink and run some water over them.

When she's next to me again our shoulders touch.

'We have to eat these while they're fresh,' I say, grabbing a knife. 'I'll show you how to shell them. The trick is to get them out without cutting your hand off.'

I slide the blade under the soft flesh and scrape it along the inside edge of the shell. The first one comes away easily.

Kas has a go, but she can't get the blade in deep enough so I put my hand over hers and push it in, then flick the flesh out. She laughs when she pushes too hard on the next one and it flies off and lands on the floor. Even when we're finished, I don't want to move. I like being here, close to her. I steal glances at her while she's not looking. Her skin is perfectly smooth and she has this habit of sliding her tongue along her lips to moisten them.

'Next step,' I say. 'Belt the shit out of them.'

'What are you saying? You're an idiot!' She's laughing again.

'Serious,' I say. 'You've got to hit them with a hammer to make them tender. Otherwise you can't eat them. Come on.'

I scoop the abs into a bucket with a bit of water and take them out to the shed. Kas follows, still thinking I'm having her on. I put them on the bench and hit them hard and fast with the hammer, one at a time. Dad and I did this for years without me ever thinking how strange it looked.

'We'll cook them now,' I say. 'We need to cut them into strips and fry them.'

Kas leans back against the bench, the last of the light catching her bare shoulders. She's still wearing the too-big singlet and all I want to do is reach out and touch her.

'You know,' she says, 'I'd been wondering how you survived here on your own for so long. I thought you must have made it up—that there was someone else here, an adult, that helped you. But you're pretty clever. And it's all stuff I don't know anything about.'

'You mean you thought I was lying?'

'No. I just thought...'

'What?'

'That you exaggerated things.'

'Well, now you know,' I say.

'Now I know.'

As I turn to walk out of the shed, she blocks my way. I try to squeeze past, but she moves and blocks me again. Then, without warning, she leans in and kisses me on the mouth. Not a soft kiss; her mouth is open and she presses her lips hard against mine. I can taste the salt on her skin and feel her hair touching my face. A couple of strands catch between our lips.

She moves away, pulls the hair back behind her ear and puts her arms around my neck. This time she pushes her whole body against me and I can feel her tongue inside my mouth. I don't know how long we kiss for. I'm not even sure if I'm still breathing. I feel myself get hard against her, but

192

I'm not embarrassed. I've never felt so alive.

At last she pulls back, but she stays so close I can feel her breathing in and out. She's smiling and I can't stop myself from smiling either. She dips her head and puts her ear to my chest. I'm sure my heart must be deafening. I loop my arms around her and we stay like this for ages, just holding each other. I lift her singlet at the back and run my fingertips over her skin, smooth and soft.

'What are you two doing?'

It's Willow, standing in the doorway.

We push apart, laughing.

'Nothing,' Kas says. 'Finn just had something in his eye and I was trying to get it out.'

'No, you weren't,' Willow says. 'You were kissing.'

'You're right,' Kas says, swooping her up in her arms. 'We were kissing.'

She burrows her face into Willow's chest, blows a raspberry against her skin and carries her out of the shed.

We fry up the abs in the kitchen, the glow of the gas jets the only light. I keep looking back at Kas at the table with Willow on her lap. When she looks at me and smiles, her teeth shine in the glow of the flame.

I try to concentrate on the cooking—I don't want to overdo them or they'll be too rubbery to eat—but all I can think of is kissing her again, feeling her body against mine.

❧

When the abs are done I put the pan in the middle of the table and we eat with our fingers, picking up the hot strips and juggling them from hand to hand to cool them. We're so hungry that no one talks. The fat drips down Kas's chin.

'So, *ladies*,' I say, in the smoothest voice I can muster up. 'What do you think about abalone?'

'It's delicious,' Willow says, picking another strip out of the pan.

'I've never tasted anything like them,' Kas says. 'They taste like the smell of the sea.'

'You wait till you try mussels,' I say. 'And oysters. Red Rocks Point is the best place for them. If we stay at Ray's for a while, I'll collect some and we'll have a feast.'

'*This* is a feast, Finn,' Kas says.

She stops eating and looks across the table at me. I can't read her expression in the shadows, but her fingers walk across the table and weave through mine.

18

We don't have time to sit and enjoy the feeling of a full belly. We have to get going.

Out in the yard, Kas slips the bridle over Yogi's head. We fill the saddlebags with tinned food, clothes and a couple of knives. Then I boost Willow onto Yogi's back and she grabs a handful of his mane.

Rowdy's excited by all the preparations. He's still favouring one of his back legs but seems happy enough to walk.

By the time we are ready to go, the moon is already high. It's almost full and I'm worried it might give too much light, but clouds begin to move in off the ocean.

'We have to cross the river,' I say.

'Okay,' Kas says. 'Let's go.'

'How's the leg?'

'All right,' she says, but I see that she's still limping heavily.

'I thought you were going to ride.'

'Yogi's got enough to carry. I'll be fine.'

We retrace our steps from the morning until we veer off to find the spot where the river has been piped under the old tip road. There's a wide verge on the side that's well concealed by the taller trees and we take the chance on following it, moving in and out of the shadows. It leads us to the intersection with the coast road, where they built the barriers when the town was quarantined. Anything burnable is long gone, but the big orange barriers are still there.

We need to follow the road for a couple of ks towards Pinchgut Junction. Then we'll turn east along the coast road leading to the top of Ray's valley.

The road is more overgrown here so we have to walk Yogi out on the last remaining strip of bitumen. His clip-clopping echoes through the bush. Rowdy lopes along on three legs next to Kas. He almost looks his old self again after a couple of good feeds.

Kas leads Yogi and I watch her silhouette: even with the limp, I love the way her body moves. Her shoulders look wider from behind and she seems to taper down to her hips. Her legs are bare below her shorts and the muscles of her calves are bunched and tight. I'm feeling things that a couple of weeks ago I thought I'd never get to feel—the need to be with a girl, to have her touch me, to kiss me.

The more time I spend with Kas, the more I notice the differences between her and Rose. She's less defensive and, even with the danger that threatens almost everywhere, she's fun to be around. From what I can make out, Rose copped the worst of what went on in Longley and she probably has every right to be less trusting. But Kas is more open, maybe more innocent. More like me, I guess.

We are still about an hour from Ray's place when Kas slows for me to catch her up.

'You know at the meeting in the valley?' she says. 'When you first saw me?'

'Yeah.'

'What'd Harry mean when he said you'd nearly killed Ramage?'

I tell her about the night at the hayshed. About the wire and cutting Ramage's hand.

'Why his hand?'

'Because that's where Rose was cut. She never said who did it, but I guessed it was Ramage.'

'Her left hand?'

'Yeah. Why?'

Kas takes my fingers and runs them over the back of her left hand. There's something hard under the skin.

'What's that?' I ask.

'It's an implant. All Sileys have them. So we could be tracked—back when there was the technology to do it.'

'So...'

'So I think she might have cut it out herself.'

'But why? They can't track you now.'

'But they can still identify us,' Kas says. 'Rose always hated it, was always picking at it. It meant you were someone else's property, bought and sold like an animal. Do you know what that feels like?'

She stops. The moonlight is behind her and it makes a halo of her hair.

'What's wrong with people in this country, Finn? Even before the virus it was so beautiful here; you had everything. But you were so cruel.'

I don't have an answer to that. We walk on in silence. There's a word on the tip of my tongue but I find it hard to let out. It's like admitting she's right, like saying we are—we always were—cruel.

'Sorry,' I say at last into the night.

Kas reaches for my hand. 'It's not your fault. It's never the kids' fault.'

The moon has almost set by the time we make it to the top of Ray's valley. To avoid getting swiped by the low branches, Willow slides down from Yogi and walks.

Finally, the trees start to thin and we come to the fence that marks the beginning of Ray's place. I know exactly where the trip-wire is so we go along to a break in the fence past the closed gate. We still can't see Ray's house from here, but as we drop down into the valley I pick out the silhouette of his roof and chimney against the night sky. There's no light and no smell of smoke.

When we get within fifty metres of the house, I whistle long and low. Ray's probably asleep. I whistle again and wait, then I hear the creak of a screen door.

'That you, young Finn?'

'Yep, it's me.'

A shadow comes out to meet us and I recognise Ray's bow-legged walk. Rowdy is already rubbing his nose against Ray's leg and Ray is scratching him under the chin.

'Jesus, Finn, I'm not runnin' a bloody guesthouse,' Ray says when he sees Kas, Willow and Yogi, but there's a chuckle in his voice. He draws me into a big bear hug.

By the time we get to the porch he's lit a small kero lamp.

'Who might these ladies be, then?'

I introduce Kas and Willow. Ray brings the lamp closer to Kas's face and nods.

'You must be Rose's sister.'

Kas can't contain herself. 'Is she here?'

'Come inside,' he says quietly.

We follow the lantern light along the hallway to the kitchen. I notice the door to one of the bedrooms is closed.

Ray hangs the lamp above the table and we sit down. Willow climbs into my lap, her eyes wide now as she takes in this new place. Ray winks at her.

'Where is she?' Kas asks.

'She's sleeping.' Ray points his chin towards the closed door.

Kas jumps to her feet, but Ray takes her by the arm.

'Let her sleep, girl. She's okay, but I have to tell you what's happened.' He leans his elbows on the table and sighs long and deep. The way the shadows fall across his face makes him look older than I remember.

'She arrived here three or four days ago,' he begins. 'In pretty bad shape. Her clothes torn, cuts all over her, and disorientated. She was feverish, too, stumbling and making no sense at all. She's crook, Finn, too crook for me to look after. I've been feeding her, but I don't have a lotta food to spare. I got her to eat some soup today, but she's just skin and bone. When she's awake she holds her belly the whole time, stroking it and talking to the baby.' Ray takes a deep breath. 'It don't look good. I reckon the baby isn't far off coming.'

'But she thought she was only six months pregnant,' I say.

'She's probably more than six months,' Kas says, and then, 'Don't ask me how I know.'

Ray goes on. 'You were right about that cut on her hand, Finn. I reckon that's where the fever has come from. The infection's spread.'

'I've got to see her,' Kas says, moving towards the door.

Ray glances at me and I nod.

'Just be real quiet,' he says. 'Sleep's the best thing for her now.'

Kas quietly opens the door off the kitchen. She starts to move through, then reaches her hand back for me.

The first thing I notice, while my eyes adjust to the dark, is the sound of Rose's breathing. It's not regular. She inhales and seems to hold her breath for ages before letting it out. Then she breathes short and sharp, like she's panting.

Kas kneels down next to the bed and puts her forehead on Rose's arm. I slip away from her grip and sit on a chair on the other side of the bed.

We stay here like this for ages. I can see Rose more clearly now from the bit of light coming through the partly opened door. She looks so small, like she's shrunk. But I can see the bulge the baby makes under the bedsheets.

Eventually Rose stirs and opens her eyes. With her right hand she reaches out and touches Kas's face. Then she turns to me and sits her other, injured, hand gently in mine.

'You found her,' she says. 'You found her.'

Her voice is so weak I can hardly hear her. Kas is crying, wiping the tears away with her sleeve.

'I think she found me,' I say.

Rose turns to Kas, pulls her in close and kisses her on the cheek. Then she takes her sister's hand and places it on her belly.

'Feel,' she says.

Kas leans in and a smile creases her lips. 'It's moving,' she says.

'We're going to be okay, aren't we, Finn?' Rose says.

'Yeah,' I say. 'Before you know it, you'll be better. You'll have the baby and we'll all move back to my place. We'll swim every day and hunt and fish and...'

'Rowdy,' Rose says suddenly. 'Did you find him?'

'He's here. He was waiting for us at home. He was hungry, but he's okay now.'

'He saved me,' she says. 'He caught me—the Wilder that stayed behind after you left—but Rowdy saved me. He attacked him.'

I want to ask about the Wilder I found dead in the paddock, the one with the arrow in his leg and the knife in his chest, but Rose's eyes are closing again and she's drifting off. She still hangs onto us, but eventually her grip loosens and we slide her hands under the sheet. Kas leans over and kisses her on the forehead. Then she kisses her belly.

Back in the kitchen, Willow has fallen asleep at the table. Kas picks her up and Ray takes them to the old couch in the lounge room.

I know we are still in danger, but everything always feels more solid, more secure, when Ray's around. It's like I can offload some of the responsibility, just for a few hours.

Ray's standing in the doorway, looking at me.

'Tough day?' he asks.

'You won't believe what's been happening.'

'Maybe in the morning, eh?' he says. 'I'm buggered, son. Not as young as I used to be. I'm going to get some shut-eye. You should too. I reckon we're all going to need our strength soon. Rose's baby is closer to coming than we thought.'

'She's not strong enough, Ray.'

'She's strong enough all right. You don't know her like I do.'

It's Kas. She's standing behind Ray in the dark.

'She's the toughest person I know.'

'I hope you're right,' Ray says.

He touches her arm as he walks past her and disappears

into his room. He comes back with some blankets.

'You'll have to kip out on the floor, you two,' he says. 'Sorry, but all the beds are taken.'

'Thanks, Ray,' I say, as he dissolves into the dark once more.

The lamplight is fading in the kitchen. Kas is just a shadow against the wall.

'I'm too wired to sleep,' I say.

'Me too. Let's sit outside for a bit.'

When she takes my hand I feel like electricity is zinging through me. I don't know how a girl can do this—make me feel so strong and helpless at the same time.

She sits on the second step of the porch and I sit behind her. She snuggles back into me and I put my arms around her. Her hands rest on mine, our fingers lacing together. We sit like this for so long I start to wonder if she has fallen asleep.

'Tell me about the sea, Finn,' she murmurs.

'What'd you mean?'

'This morning, at the rock pools. I saw the way you were with it.'

'When I wasn't perving at you, you mean?'

'Ha.' She nudges me and falls quiet again.

'It's hard to explain,' I say, searching for the words. 'I grew up with it. Dad taught me to surf when I was about eight. It probably sounds strange, but for me it's always been about being in that great big ocean, feeling it move under me, understanding how powerful it is, how I'm just a cork bobbing in the hugeness of it.'

Kas turns her head to look at me, resting her chin on my arm.

'It's stupid,' I say, 'but I used to dream I'd grown gills and I could stay underwater for as long I wanted.'

'It's not stupid at all. But I want to know—what's it like to ride a wave.'

'I guess it's what it must be like to ride a horse at full gallop,' I say. 'You're just moving with the energy of something so much bigger and stronger than you, something that could crush you if it wanted to, but for those few seconds you're sharing the energy.'

Kas nods. 'I know that feeling. I used to have a horse no one else could ride. Stan called him Brutus, but I had my own name for him. River. We just connected somehow, he knew I was never going to hurt him and I believed he'd never hurt me either.'

Ray's back porch looks down the valley to the woodshed and the bush beyond it. The wind has dropped right away and the moon has long since set. The clouds have cleared too and the night sky is speckled with stars.

Kas leans back into me, lifts my hand and brushes my fingers against her face. I know she's tracing her birthmark with my fingertips.

'You know, back there in the logging coup? Yesterday?' she says.

'Yeah.'

'You said I was—'

'—beautiful.'

'No one's ever told me that. No one. Not even Stan and Beth. They always said it was such a shame that I was born this way. But...'

'But what?'

'It's the way I am. It's me.'

She's holding the palm of my hand against her face now, over her birthmark.

'I meant it,' I say. 'You're beautiful. I've never known a girl like you.'

'Yeah, well, there's not that many girls to choose from anymore.'

'It's not just that. You're fierce and strong and you fight when you have to. And you're a bit scary. I saw what you did to Tusker!'

'So,' she says, turning around and facing me, 'do you want to fight me or...?'

Her lips are against mine again and she's pressing her whole body into me. Her arms are looped around my neck and her tongue is pushing into my mouth. I take her face in my hands and hold her there, thinking I never want her to stop doing just what she's doing right now. She pulls her head back and looks straight at me, then she brushes her lips against mine again and again. Even in the dark, I see her smile.

'You're a good kisser,' she says softly. 'I bet you had plenty of girlfriends.'

'I've only ever kissed two girls. And I wouldn't call them girlfriends. I was only thirteen. What about you?'

Her silence tells me I shouldn't have brought it up.

'Sorry.'

'It's okay.' She sighs. 'The thing is, I wasn't allowed off the farm unless I was with Stan or Beth, and most of the time I wouldn't go into town even if they asked me. There was a boy from the next property, Charlie Gunn, who used to come over to help Stan with the crutching, but he was much more interested in Rose than me. I was just the kid sister who hung around. But one afternoon he came over when Rose was in town with Stan. Charlie and I were sorting fleeces in the woolshed and he kissed me. He told me I would be as pretty as Rose if I didn't have my birthmark.'

Kas gets to her feet and pulls me up by the hand.

'Let's get the blankets,' she says. 'We can sleep out here on the porch.'

We tiptoe around the kitchen. It still smells of the kero lamp. Kas looks in on Rose. I pick up the blankets and we both head back out onto the porch.

'She's still sleeping,' Kas says.

We spread two blankets one on top of the other to lie on, and pull the third over us. It's not exactly warm, but Kas snuggles in next to me. Her hair has a musky smell and I can feel her breath on my skin. She turns her head up and kisses me, not on the lips but on the side of my face.

'I feel safe with you,' she says.

She pushes in closer and her body moulds to mine. Her breathing gets slower and deeper. I relax and try to sleep too, but the events of the day keep flashing through my head. I keep coming back to being here with Kas, her body so close and warm, Rose asleep inside, Ray and Willow and Rowdy, all of us together now, like a family. And that feeling somehow keeps the thought of danger at bay.

19

'Finn!'

I wake in the half-light to find Ray leaning over and shaking me. Kas stirs too and we both look up at him, trying to make sense of what's going on.

'You'd better come in,' he says. 'It's Rose.'

We scramble up and straightaway the cold morning air hits me. I can still feel Kas's warmth where she's been lying against my back.

She keeps hold of my hand as we walk through into the kitchen. The sun isn't up yet, but there's enough morning light in the house for us to see. Ray's got the lamp in Rose's bedroom, filling it with a dull light.

She's lying back on her elbows with her head up and a look of disbelief on her face. The sheets are wet. Not just perspiration wet, they're saturated.

'Her waters have broken,' Ray says.

I'm not exactly sure what that means, but I figure it can't be good.

'The baby's coming,' he explains.

Kas kneels down next to Rose and tucks her sister's wet hair back behind her ears.

'You okay?' she asks.

Rose is more alert than she was last night, but I can tell she's scared.

'It's too soon,' she says. 'It's too soon.'

'We don't know that, Rose.' Ray's voice is solid, careful. 'It could be perfectly normal for all we know. You could be due.'

'Fuck!' Rose says and her head drops back into the pillows.

'All right, you two,' Ray says to Kas and me. 'We've gotta be as prepared as we can. We'll need clean water and you'll find some towels in the cupboard in the hallway.'

I'm not sure if he actually knows what he's doing or if he's remembering some old movie he saw years ago. Either way, I'm just happy to have someone else making the decisions.

Kas and I are getting everything organised in the kitchen when we hear a low growl that progresses to a long *aaah* sound.

'It's a contraction,' Kas says. 'Get used to the noise, there's going to be a lot more of it.'

'How do you know about that?' I ask.

'The feedstore. There was a girl that had a baby. She was younger than Rose. I helped.'

'You need to tell Ray,' I say.

She heads back into the bedroom and I hear their short conversation. Ray goes through to the lounge room and returns with a thick book under his arm. He puts it down on the table.

'Remember I told you about this?' he says. 'It's an old textbook of Harriet's. There's a section on births.'

He bustles out to the porch and returns with another kero lamp, which he lights and places on the table.

'I'm gonna help Kas,' he says. 'Find the right page and start reading, son. We'll need all the information we can get.'

I hold the book up. *Human Anatomy and Physiology*. I flick to the index and find Chapter 17, 'The Stages of Labour', and start reading.

'Ray,' I say. He sticks his head around the door. 'We need to time the contractions.'

'You'd better start counting,' he says.

Kas comes back out and sits down next to me. She loops her arm through mine and starts to read too.

'Rose says she's been having little contractions all night. That was the first big one, though.'

'How is she?' I ask.

'It's hard to tell. She's not making a lot of sense—and that's a worry. When the contractions get really heavy she'll have to concentrate on her breathing and try to keep it together. It could take hours or it could happen quickly. Everyone's different.'

'What about the girl at the feedstore?'

'Danka was another Siley. She was my best friend in there. We were the same age, but she was really pretty. I think she was happy when she got pregnant—meant she didn't have to work as much. It took about twelve hours for her baby to come.'

I turn the page and there are diagrams of a baby being born. It all looks so clean and neat in the pictures.

'Rose is tough,' Kas says, 'but she's sick. I've never seen her this thin.'

Willow wanders into the kitchen, rubbing the sleep from her eyes. She climbs onto Kas's lap.

'Is Rose going to have a baby?' Willow asks.

'Yes, she is,' I say.

Rose moans loudly. Kas pushes Willow off, jumps up, and goes into the bedroom.

The moans become louder, broken by short periods of silence. I can hear Rose's loud intakes of air before more low groans. Willow buries her face in my jumper and covers her ears.

Ray comes and sits opposite us. He looks so much older, his face more grizzled.

I ask Willow to go and give Rowdy some food out on the porch. Ray follows her with a plate of bones.

When we're alone again, with just the sound of Rose's contractions in the next room, I ask Ray if Rose told him anything about the dead man I found in the paddock on Parker Street.

'He had an arrow in the back of his leg,' I explain, 'and a knife sticking out of his chest. It was one of our kitchen knives.'

'She said there'd been a fight, but she didn't tell me about killing anyone.' He scratches the bristles on his chin. 'She's as fierce as they come. I can only guess what they did to her up there at Longley, but whatever it was she'll do anything not to go back.'

'She was protecting us too. She knew the Wilder had found my place. He had to be kept silent.'

'Well, he can't get any more silent than that.'

There's a louder, longer groan from the bedroom and I hear Kas telling Rose to breathe. The contractions are getting closer together. We've got everything ready: basins for warm water, plenty of towels and a couple of big cushions for Rose if she needs to get into a more comfortable position. Ray has lit a fire in the combustion stove.

'We're all going to have to help in there, Finn,' he says. 'You as well.'

'But I don't know what to do, Ray.'

'She's gonna scream the house down most likely. Harriet used to say childbirth was like trying to push a basketball through a garden hose. I went with her once, over to Brigid Watson's place. They had the next farm over. It was when there were no doctors left on the coast. Her husband had died and her kids were just young'uns, so they weren't much help. Strongest woman I ever seen. She ran that farm on her own, even while she was pregnant. Harriet said she had child-bearing hips.'

'What's that mean?'

'A big arse, I reckon. Anyway, the baby slipped out like toothpaste from a tube. Cute little bugger, too. Girl. Didn't live past her first birthday, though. But I watched what Harriet did, getting Brigid comfortable, talking to her the whole time. Reassuring her. Brigid delivered the baby on all fours.'

I'm starting to feel a bit sick with this detail, but at least I know more of what to expect.

'Rose doesn't have child-bearing hips,' I say.

'No, she doesn't, son. But she's got youth on her side.'

Kas, Ray and I spend the day and most of the night taking it in turns to sit with Rose, trying to reassure her. The contractions gradually grow more intense, longer and closer together.

It must be well after midnight when Ray lights the lamp and brings it back into the bedroom. The brightness seems to startle Rose, who hasn't said much, apart from swearing, for a while. But with the light she becomes more lucid.

Between the contractions I wipe the sweat off her face and rub her back. She surprises me when she leans into my shoulder and puts her arm around my neck.

'Hey, dog boy,' she whispers.

'Hey,' I say. 'How you feeling?'

'Like shit. Feels like a pony kicking around inside me.'

'You'll be okay,' I say, trying to convince myself as much as her. 'You'll *both* be okay.'

'If...'

'If what?'

'Promise me you and Kas will...'

'We'll all look after the baby together,' I say. 'You and me and Kas and Ray and Willow. All of us. We're a family now.'

212

'A family?' Her face softens. 'It's a long time since I had a family.'

'Well, you've got one now.'

She looks at me. Her eyes are still red and her face is flushed. 'Thanks for finding Kas,' she says. 'She told me a bit about what happened.'

'She's as tough as you, your sister.'

'Tougher, I reckon.'

Exhausted again, she falls back onto the pillow.

'Keep talking, Finn,' she whispers. 'I like to hear your voice.'

'About what?'

'Anything. Like you talked to me in the kitchen that first day.'

'Growly, you mean?'

'Ha. No, not so growly.'

'I like Kas,' I say. 'She's fierce, but she's got a soft side, too.'

It doesn't take long before the next contraction swells and takes over her whole body. It's like she's losing the strength to deal with each new one.

She rolls onto her side, then slowly lifts herself up onto her hands and knees. Her mouth is pulled tight and her knees are shaking. She lets out a scream.

'Get Kas,' she gasps. 'And Ray.'

I don't need to call them; they've both heard the scream. Rose buries her head in the pillow and her hips sway from side to side. The contractions are so close together now; she hardly has time to recover from one when the next one hits. Sweat drips from her face to her chest.

Rose stands behind her sister and, at the next contraction, gasps.

'I can see the head! I can see the head!'

But Rose slumps forwards, her head hitting the bedend. Kas holds her by the hips and lifts her off her stomach.

'Rose,' she urges, 'you're nearly there. When the next contraction comes, push with everything you've got.'

Rose's voice is low, drained. 'I can't.'

'You can. I know you can,' Kas says. 'It'll be over soon. I promise.'

Kas looks at Ray and me and mouths *Help*.

'Come round here,' Ray says, taking my arm. He gets me to kneel on the bed in front of Rose so she can put her arms over my shoulders for support. She pushes her forehead hard into my chest. When she looks up I can see her eyes rolling around, as though she's struggling to stay conscious. When the next contraction grips her, she digs her hands into my back and screams.

'That's good, Rose. Good. The head is coming,' Kas says. I can hear the control in her voice. 'Push. *Push*.'

But Rose has gone limp in my arms. Her breath is coming in short bursts. Her whole weight is falling into me. I take her face in my hands and bring it close to mine.

'Come on, Rose, one more push,' I say.

Her eyes flicker open. Then she draws herself up and her body tenses again before she bears down and all her remaining energy goes into a scream that's so close I can feel it.

'One more, one more.' Kas is shouting now.

214

But Rose's arms have fallen off my shoulders and her head rolls away to the side. I turn her face towards me and gently slap her cheek.

'Stay with us, Rose,' I say. 'Stay with us. Please…'

I put my face against hers. My tears mix with the saltiness of her sweat.

'I think she's unconscious,' I hear myself say.

'Gravity,' Ray says. 'We've gotta use gravity.' He pulls Rose around to the side of the bed, kneels down and takes her weight on his shoulders. 'When I lift,' he tells Kas, 'you're going to have to pull. We've gotta get the baby out. Finn, help me lift her.'

I slip in under him and take some of the weight in my arms.

'Now,' he says. '*Now!*'

I see the head between Rose's legs. Kas is pulling and turning. I see the shoulders and then the whole body slips out into her hands.

Ray eases Rose back down onto the bed just as the baby cries.

'It's a girl,' Kas says, tears streaming down her cheeks. 'It's a girl.'

Ray has a piece of string, which he ties around the umbilical cord, then produces another piece and ties that around too. Kas has a pair of scissors and she cuts the cord. Then she wraps the baby in a towel.

When we gently roll Rose over we see the blood. It's falling in big drops onto the sheets.

'She's hemorrhaging,' Ray says. He bundles up a towel and puts it between Rose's legs. 'I don't know how to stop it.'

Kas has the baby wrapped up and she kneels down next

to Rose, nuzzling the baby's face against Rose's. I don't know whether I imagine it, but I'm sure I see a smile on Rose's lips. Her whole body is limp. I'm not sure she's even breathing.

Ray takes the baby and hands her to me, then he puts his head to Rose's chest and listens. He tilts her head back and begins to give her mouth-to-mouth.

Kas lifts her sister's hand to her face, kisses it and whispers, 'Don't leave me, Rose. Don't leave me.'

Ray starts to press up and down on her chest, but her body is so small and wasted he's afraid to push too hard. The towel between her legs is soaked with blood.

After a few minutes Ray checks for breathing again. There's nothing. He keeps trying, but eventually he has to stop.

Kas climbs onto the bed and cradles Rose's head in her lap. I hand her the baby and she holds her against her sister's breast. Ray looks at me and nods towards the door.

Back out in the kitchen, Willow is sitting with Rowdy in his basket, her eyes wide.

'Is there a baby?' she asks.

I scoop her up in my arms because I just want someone to hug. 'Yes. A little girl.'

Ray sits at the table with his head resting on his arms. It's been a long night.

I feel numb. It's like the world has overtaken me and I want to scream and yell at God or the sky. I want to say it's not fair. I want to say we're only kids and we shouldn't have to deal with this stuff, that there should be more adults like Ray to help us.

But all I can do is rock Willow in my arms. I can't even cry anymore. I've been hollowed out and there's nothing left. I think of Mum and Dad dying and of the hole they left in my life. It shouldn't keep happening, I've had my fair share. It's someone else's turn.

There's a faint sound coming from the bedroom, a cooing, encouraging voice: Kas talking to the baby. I take Willow to the door. She wants to see the baby. But when I'm in the doorway, Ray's voice cuts through the house, urgent.

'Finn!'

I turn back around to see light out through the kitchen window. It takes me a second to work out it's a flaming torch. And not just one—there are four of them crossing the paddock towards the house. And then, a noise that starts like a buzzing in the back of my head. Slowly it increases until I realise what it is.

A trailbike.

20

Ray moves quickly. In the bedroom he pushes a bookshelf to one side revealing a cavity behind it.

'Quick,' he says. 'Get in here. Take Willow.'

He lifts Kas off the bed. She tries to push him away, not understanding what's going on, but he takes the baby from her arms, guides her to the cavity and pushes her in after Willow.

'You can't do this on your own, Ray,' I say. 'I'm not hiding.'

He takes me by the shoulders. 'It's you three they want,' he says. 'They won't take the baby and Rose is...' He stops and looks at her on the bed.

'But what about you?'

'I'm too old for them to worry about,' he says, and points at the cavity. 'Now get in there.'

There's just enough room for three. It's musty and smells of rats. Most of the light is blocked when Ray pushes the bookshelf back into place, but if I flatten myself against the side wall I can see through a small gap into the room. Ray sits himself down on the bed, cradling the baby in his arms. Waiting.

Slowly the room fills with light and large shadows. No one has said anything, but I can see Ray looking up at a man standing in the doorway. His large shape moves around to the other side of the bed and he drops to his knees.

It's Ramage.

He reaches out and touches Rose on the cheek. When his voice comes, it's thin and low.

'Ah, Warda, my beautiful Warda. Why did you run? I could have looked after you.'

Kas is pressed against me. She's heard the voice and knows who it is.

Ramage reaches out to Ray—to the baby.

'This is Rose's daughter,' Ray says, shaking his head. '*Rose's*.'

'Warda is my Siley. The child is mine.'

Ray looks to the door as someone else enters the room, someone smaller than Ramage. They come closer to Ray and reach for the baby.

'It's okay,' a woman's voice says, 'I'll look after her.'

Through the gap, I can see her flaming red hair and I remember Rose's description of the woman who saved her when she was caught at Swan's Marsh. It must be the same woman.

Her voice is gentle. 'Has she fed?' she asks.

'No,' Ray mumbles.

Ramage leans over the bed and softly kisses Rose. Then stands to his full height and guides the woman out of the room. When he comes back, his voice is hard again, and angry.

'The sister,' he says, 'and the boy. Where are they?'

Ray is ready for the question. He answers without hesitating.

'They *were* here,' he says. 'They're gone now. Left a couple of hours ago.'

'Gone?' Ramage sounds unconvinced. 'Gone where?'

'Didn't say.'

'Don't you lie to me, you old prick.'

'Why would I lie?' Ray speaks in an older, weary voice. 'What've I got to gain from lying?' He straightens and stands toe to toe with Ramage.

'If I find you've lied to me,' Ramage says, 'I'll burn ya fuckin' house down.' He turns and yells, 'Search the place. Tear it apart. If she's here, we'll find her. And the boy. I'll kill him.'

I can feel Willow trembling beside me. I draw her in and hold her head against my chest. Kas's arm loops over us both and we huddle together and wait.

Heavy footsteps come through the back door and the room fills with light and the smell of burning pitch. Tables and chairs are being turned over, but above the ruckus I hear the woman's voice, loud and clear.

'Stop!'

Ramage turns and I know she's looking straight at him.

'There's no time for this,' she says. 'This baby's premature. If you want her to survive we've got to get her back home as soon as we can. The mother's dead. That's enough tragedy for one day.'

Ramage hesitates before stabbing his finger into Ray's chest.

'I know where to find you, old man. Any more trouble from down here and I'll be back. And you tell that girl and boy that I don't forget. Benny Ramage never forgets. They'll *never* be safe. Not here. Not anywhere.'

Ramage leans over the bed one more time and kisses Rose. Then he pushes past Ray, knocking him against the bookshelf. Footsteps thump out through the kitchen and onto the porch.

Ray waits a good fifteen minutes before he pushes the bookshelf out of the way and we crawl out into the bedroom. He has his finger to his lips.

'I don't trust them,' he says. 'They'll still be watching.'

But there's no sign of their torches in the grey light of the new day. Ray gathers us all in the kitchen.

'You have to go now,' he says, 'before it gets proper light. Head down the valley to the coast and make your way back to Angowrie. Be careful.'

'I'm not running,' Kas says, her voice low but firm. 'I'm not leaving Rose. What about her...her *body*?'

'I'll look after her, I promise,' Ray says. 'There's nothing to be gained from you being caught by Ramage.' He's got his hand on Kas's shoulder. 'You'd best go in and say your goodbyes.'

Kas looks bewildered, torn, raking a hand through her hair.

'Ray's right,' I say, softly. 'We have to go.'

Kas takes my hand and leads me into the bedroom, to Rose. She leans over until her forehead rests on her sister's. As she does, her mother's ring slips out of her shirt and falls onto Rose's chest.

'I promise you,' she whispers, 'I promise you I'll find your baby.'

Kas straightens and turns to me. 'The baby needs a name,' she says.

I don't know why the answer comes so quickly, but it's as though the name has been there, waiting to be spoken.

'Hope,' I say. 'Let's call her Hope.'

Ray is standing at the door. 'Come on, you have to go,' he says, urgent again. 'It's getting lighter.'

Kas kisses Rose a final time before backing away into the kitchen.

I'm left alone with Rose. Her face is cold when I touch it. I kneel down by the bed and put my head on the pillow next to hers.

'Hey,' I say. 'It's me, dog boy. I'm sorry I couldn't look after you better.' My eyes cloud with tears. 'But I promise I'll look after Kas. And we'll find Hope and bring her home so she can swim in the sea. And I'll teach her to surf. But I've got to go now. I've got to go, Rose.'

I roll her name around in my mouth like I did the night I met her.

Kas has pulled an old coat around Willow's shoulders and has hitched her onto her back. Ray hands me a small bag with some food.

'When you reach Red Rocks Point, check the tide,' he says. 'If it's low enough, follow the beach all the way back into town. You can't risk the cliff tops track. They might be watching it. Leave the horse here, but take Rowdy with you. Wait for a week then come back to me. Catch me a couple of bunnies, if you can. I've been missing them.'

I put my arms around him. He waits a couple of seconds before saying, gruff-like and embarrassed, 'All right, enough of that now. You've got to get moving.'

Kas hardly seems to realise what's going on. She walks straight out the door and I have to grab her arm before she breaks cover.

'Wait,' I say. She turns and looks at me with blank eyes. 'We've got to keep low, Kas. They could still be out there.'

I take Willow off her back and hand her the bag. Rowdy is standing on the top step of the porch, sniffing the wind. He seems unconcerned; I take that as a good sign.

We run across the home paddock to the shed. Even pulling Willow along, I'm faster than Kas, who is still limping. After we've cleared the fence, we walk through the bush in silence, all the way down to Red Rocks Point.

By the time we reach the first of the big granite slabs, the sun has risen and is warming our backs. Rowdy is restless. He knows we're going home, but the tide is too high for us to get all the way along the base of the cliffs to the river mouth. By the look of the wet sand further up the beach, the tide is dropping.

We find a nook where we can't be seen. Kas sits with her back to the rock. Her head is up, but her eyes are closed. I sit next to her. Little tremors run through her body and she swipes at her tears with the back of her hand.

'It's not fair, Finn,' she says, finally. 'It's not fair. She didn't do anything wrong. Everything she did was to protect me.'

I kick at a loose stone. 'Nothing's fair,' I mutter. 'Nothing's been fair since the virus. None of the old rules apply anymore.'

She turns her head away and catches a tear before it falls.

'It's *never* been fair for Rose and me—not even before the virus.'

She balls her hand into a fist and hits the granite again and again, until I grab her arm and pull her into me. Big sobs wrack her body and I feel every one of them against my chest.

By mid-morning the tide has dropped, allowing us to make our way back along the beach to Angowrie. It's a beautiful day, with the sun glistening off the water and a regular swell breaking on the sandbars.

Looking at the waves shaping up and peeling left and right takes my mind off the pain I feel in my body. And the ache in the middle of my chest. Kas walks a few steps behind me.

It takes us a couple of hours to reach the river mouth. The low tide means we can wade across, but we check for danger first. I scout upriver until I can see the road bridge, but there's no sign of life. The Wilders' camp on the other bank is deserted.

Crossing the water, Willow on my back and Kas by my side, I try to remember how long ago it was that Rose and I waded over to escape from Ramage. However long it is, I wish I could go back and have that time again. I'd have done things differently; I'd have kept Rose safe.

When we reach the other bank, Kas walks ahead, her wet clothes clinging to her body. In all the drama of the last few hours, I'd almost forgotten how close we've grown to each other, forgotten that we've kissed and kept each other warm through the night.

But all that's been buried under the weight of losing Rose. Just like when Dad died, and then Mum, it'll take time for everything to sink in and for us to work out what to do next. Willow needs to be looked after and there's still the matter of staying alive, finding food, keeping safe. Maybe it'll be weeks, months even, but somewhere in all of that, Kas and me will find some space to talk about us.

21

Winter is starting to push in, the first storm hitting Angowrie last night. I'd forgotten the noise the town makes in the wind, the gates left open to swing and creak, all the loose roofing iron banging where the screws have rusted out. In a way, we don't mind the bad weather. It will push the Wilders back to Longley and hopefully keep them there for the winter.

Kas has spent the last few days moving in slow motion. I see small sparks in her when she's playing with Willow, a smile that escapes without her realising, or the way she scoops her hair behind her ear and looks up at me sometimes. Every now and again she brushes past, maybe deliberately, maybe because we are so cramped in the house, but each time I reach out to hold her, she's gone. I feel the loss of Rose too, but compared to Kas I hardly knew her.

Kas sleeps with Willow and sometimes I hear her crying in the night. In the mornings she looks as though she's hardly slept, her eyes red and her hair matted. Willow seems to have a way through to her that I don't. She crawls onto Kas's lap and snuggles into her chest. Sometimes I wish I could do the same, to feel her body against mine again, to hold her and make the pain go away, even just for a while.

I started hunting the day after we got back from Ray's. We needed fresh meat and fish but, if I'm honest, I wanted to get back into some sort of routine too. There's comfort in it, doing what I know best without having to think about it.

Whenever I head out, I ask Kas if she wants to join me. She never does. Willow has become my shadow, though; she likes getting out of the house, no matter how bad the weather. The ocean is too churned up for me to dive, but we can usually get some crabs out on the reef, and there are always rabbits to be caught.

The traps were where I'd left them, hidden in the hollow log up by the fences. I brought them back home and greased them, making sure the plates and springs were easy to set. Then I fell back into my old pattern of laying the traps in the evenings and rising early to check them in the mornings. If it wasn't for Willow padding along behind me, I could almost believe it was just Rowdy and me again, the two of us keeping each other company, skirting around the back of the golf course and climbing the ridge to the fence lines. But I know there will be no going back to that life—everything changed the day Rose arrived.

The first rabbit stew I cook draws Kas out of her room. The smell fills the house. We haven't had any fresh food since the abalone I caught before we went to Ray's.

When the rabbit's cooked we sit around the table and eat, slurping and crunching our way to the bottom of the pot. I think it's one of the best meals I've ever eaten. The wind is howling outside, and every few minutes squalls batter the roof with hailstones.

When she's finished, Kas pushes back her chair and crosses her arms. She hardly speaks now, so it surprises me when she says, 'I've been thinking...'

'What?' I ask.

'Do you reckon Ramage would have made it back to Longley?'

'He had the trailbike. He could have taken Hope and that woman with him. The rest of the Wilders could have followed. If these storms keep up no one'll be crossing the range for a couple of months at least.'

'We need to wait out the winter,' she says, her voice loud against the hail. 'Then...'

I've known this was coming, I just didn't expect it so soon. 'Then what?'

'Find Hope and bring her back here,' she says, the old steel-iness returning to her voice.

'And what about Ramage?'

She clenches her fists and plants them on the table.

'I'm going to hunt him down and kill him.'

The hail begins to ease to a steady rain.

'You don't have to come if you don't want to,' she adds.

Somehow my answer is made simpler because I know I won't have to act on it straightaway. It'll be months before we can travel.

'If you're going, I'm going too,' I say, avoiding her eyes.

In the morning I paddle out for the first time in weeks. The storm has backed off, but I know the next front won't be far away. With each duck dive and the feeling of the familiar surge underneath me, it's as though the events of the last month, the fear and the love and the death, are all washed clean, at least for a while.

Rowdy keeps watch on the beach, chasing seagulls and snapping at the whitewater like it's something he can catch. The swell is small but clean, and I surf wave after wave, each one bringing me closer to that balance that's been missing since the day Rose arrived—a balance that doesn't seem to exist on land anymore. Like it always does, the ocean stops time and only the exhaustion in my arms and shoulders tells me it's time to paddle in.

Rowdy bounds out through the shore break to meet me, and I see two familiar figures sitting halfway up the dune. They rise slowly to their feet and walk down to the beach, their feet sinking in the soft, dry sand.

As they come closer, Willow does a cartwheel, her blonde

hair flying in the wind. Kas hangs back, her eyes following each wave as it makes its way into the river mouth.

'D'you reckon you could teach me how to do that?' she asks.

ACKNOWLEDGMENTS

This book has felt like a collaboration from the beginning—so many people have invested their time, energy and faith in it. My thanks firstly to the members of each of the writing groups I have been part of over the last four years—I am lucky to have been surrounded by such talented writers and readers. Special thanks to Melanie Cheng and Terry Gunn, who read the early drafts and helped in the development of the manuscript. To my YA trial readers Scarlett Murray, Jesse Stapleton and Chloe Schneider who convinced me I was on the right track and provided invaluable feedback on how to make it better. Thanks also to the other writers who have contributed along the way—Amber Woodward, Michelle Wright, Siobhan Sheridan and Michelle Irving.

To my wonderful local supporters Nicole Maher and Nan McNab, who have been unfailingly encouraging and supportive; to Toni Jordan for her assistance and advice in developing the manuscript; to Favel Parrett, who took the time to give me the benefit of her experience when I needed it; to all the editors of the journals, magazines and anthologies who saw enough in my writing to take a chance on publishing it (especially Jock Serong and Mick Sowry from *Great Ocean Quarterly*, still my favourite layout and story!); to Caroline Wood and Margaret River Press for the use of the beautiful studio at Margaret River; to Anna, Jason, Harriet and Matilda for my writing home-away-from-home at Falmouth; to all at Writers Victoria who do so much to nurture and develop writers in this state; and to Amanda Lohrey for the wise counsel and long chats in her kitchen.

Thanks also to the whole team at Text—from the staff member who picked a raw manuscript off the slush pile, read it and actually liked it, to Rebecca Starford for her calm, no-fuss editing, to Steph Speight, Jane Pearson and Kirsty Wilson.

Above all, to my family, who make it all possible by creating time for me to write and who constantly nourish and support me in every aspect of my life—Lynne, Oliver, Maddy and Harley. They're keepers, the lot of them.

And finally, to my parents, June and Bert, who blessed me with a childhood not unlike Finn's, with the freedom to roam, explore, discover and learn.

GUARANTEED GREAT READ— OR YOUR MONEY BACK

If you bought Mark Smith's *The Road to Winter* and didn't find it a great read, here's what to do:

Remove the front cover, write your name and address below and send the cover and this page to:

The Text Publishing Company
Swann House, 22 William Street
Melbourne VIC 3000
Australia

Name _____

Address _____

_____ Postcode_____

Daytime phone number_____

Please enclose your bookshop receipt

Please allow up to eight weeks for your refund. Refunds are only payable if this page, the cover and original proof of purchase are provided. Expires 31 December 2016.